Tit'

The Wooden Bicycle
and Other Stories

Tikum Mbah Azonga

Langaa Research & Publishing CIG
Mankon, Bamenda

Publisher:
Langaa RPCIG
Langaa Research & Publishing Common Initiative Group
P.O. Box 902 Mankon
Bamenda
North West Region
Cameroon
Langaagrp@gmail.com
www.langaa-rpcig.net

Distributed outside N. America by African Books Collective
orders@africanbookscollective.com
www.africanbookscollective.com

Distributed in N. America by Michigan State University Press
msupress@msu.edu
www.msupress.msu.edu

ISBN: 9956-558-35-4

DISCLAIMER

The names, characters, places and incidents in this book are either the product of the author's imagination or are used fictitiously. Accordingly, any resemblance to actual persons, living or dead, events, or locales is entirely one of incredible coincidence.

The Wooden Bicycle and Other Stories

Contents

1

The Wooden Bicycle

There are times when despite the feelings parents may have for a child, they still wish they had not brought that particular child to life. Such was the case with Jonas Bikwibili and his son, Moses. He was the first of seven children Jonas had with his wife, Judith.

Moses was 13, and now in Class Seven, the final class in primary school. If all went well, that is, if he passed both the First School Leaving Certificate Exam (FSLC) and the Common Entrance Exam into Secondary School, he would gain a place in college. It was his father's greatest wish that the boy should pass the entrance in List 'A' in order to gain an automatic government scholarship. If he didn't make it, things would definitely be difficult, for his father depended very much on his coffee farm. But for some years now, harvests had been poor, and it was clear he would not be able to afford the boy's school fees.

The two hardly ever saw eye-to-eye, for, Jonas often said of his son that he had 'a certain madness' which he didn't like. He called him a devil and an unworthy son. Perhaps this was because being a hard working man himself; he couldn't bear to see a lazy son. Moses' "madness," Jonas said, consisted of wasting valuable time, carving he knew not what out of wood which his mother would have used for cooking.

But the boy always said he was "producing" a bicycle. He carved two wheels, a large one for the back of his bicycle and a smaller one for the front. Several times his father

1

smashed the bicycle before it was completed. "Is this not madness, for God's sake? Aren't you just stupid? Have you even seen a bicycle made of wood? Instead of revising your school work, or helping your mother, or even looking after the younger ones, you keep carving nonsense!"

But disapproval from his father never dampened the boy's spirits in his craft. It is true that he never really gave his school work all the attention it needed, although of course, he always passed his exams. But his teachers just like parents, were deeply concerned about his performance. No doubt his teacher had commented on his end-of-term report card: "an intelligent boy who could do better." Clearly, his bicycle business was like an obsession although his father beat him every so often. Moses would steal himself away to work on the bicycle. As might be expected, because of the repeated threats from his father, he moved his tools away from the latter's compound to a thicket near one of his mother's farms , situated about a kilometre away. Once she had run into this hiding place of his, but although he wasn't there at the time, she hadn't any doubt that this was a place of her son's making. But she never mentioned this to Moses or his father. She had a soft spot in her heart for her children whom she said she had borne all alone. "A father can bear to beat a child the way he likes, for he knows not what bringing forth one involves," she would say. All she told Moses was that he should do his household chores and take his studies seriously.

The time for his exams came and he sat for both the FSLC and Common Entrance. The schools broke up for the long holidays. If all went well, he would be going to college, and hopefully on government scholarship when the new academic year started in three months' time. Even so, his father had great doubts about his prospects. How could a child who spent his time on pointless and fruitless activities ever do well in his exams, he wondered aloud. Moses' mother for her part, in her heart of hearts had one prayer: "Lord, you made me and you gave me this child. If what he is doing is right, let him continue; if it is wrong, may you stop him."

During the holidays, Moses worked even harder on his craft. But he made sure he did his chores such that his parents had no reason to complain. When he completed the bicycle he took it out for testing. It was on a Sunday evening when there was some laxity in practically all families. This was the day on which no one went to the farms, but on which inter-family meetings of all sorts took place and during which children were free to play together. Moses was with Teboh, his immediate younger brother, aged 11. He needed Teboh to push the bicycle uphill so that it could be ridden on its own. As far as the bicycle was concerned, the village was ideal because it had a long stretch of some four kilometres of low gradient road. When Moses was ready to embark on the downward journey, he swung the bicycle round and asked his junior brother to jump on the back seat. Moses held the steering frame firmly, and then released the foot brake and his bicycle started rolling down.

"If Moses doesn't pass the Common Entrance in List 'A' and therefore doesn't obtain the government scholarship, what we shall do?" his mother was asking his father back at home.

"That's a good question. Well, I suppose we'll keep him at home so that he can try again next year, because I honestly don't see how we can afford the eighty thousand francs he needs for the year's school fees. And there are the other children who also need fees, books, uniforms and all the rest. They are still in primary school, which fortunately means that they don't need as much as Moses, but then we have five in primary school; excluding Mary who is only a year old, which still makes the total amount substantial."

"Don't worry. God will provide."

"That's what you always say. Anyway, let's hope he will."

Just then, Moses and Teboh came running into the compound. No one can say how long it took them to cover the three kilometres to the compound. They themselves couldn't say. All Moses knew was that they r-a-a-n! They were out of breath, but he manages to speak.

"Where is Papa? Where is …"

"What's the matter, my child? You have both been running! Was anyone chasing you?" Judith asked as she caught Moses in her arms.

"Where is Papa?" He repeated.

"Yes, Moses. What's the matter? He responded, emerging from the sitting room.

All the boy did was to remove a bundle of CFA bank notes from his pocket, which he held out to his father.

"What! Where did you get all this money from?" he asked, overwhelmed.

"The wooden bicycle," he gasped.

"The what? What is the meaning of all this, Judith?" he turned to his wife.

"How should I know? Why don't you ask him?"

"It's the wooden bicycle, Papa. The white man who owns the large shoe company in town bought it. He was here and saw Teboh and me riding the bicycle, and …"

"What bicycle are you talking about? That thing I destroyed?"

"Yes; I made another one"

"What! And he bought it for eighty thousand francs?"

"No, he asked me how much I would sell it for and when I told him one hundred and fifty thousand francs, he did not argue. He told me I should bring my father to his office tomorrow morning where the remaining seventy thousand francs will be paid."

"I can't believe this," he said, counting the money. "My son, tell me how it all happened."

"I was descending the Mbon Hill with Teboh at the back when an approaching car stopped. Then the white man got out of the car with a white girl. They looked at us ride past with a lot of admiration. Then he asked us to stop. He got the bicycle, rode it, examined it closely and said to the girl: "This is great!" He told us that his daughter had come from the country on holidays from America and that she was doing a project on children's toys in Africa. He offered to buy the bicycle so that his daughter could take it home and show it to her university."

"Wonderful! Is that so, my son?" Jonas exclaimed. Meanwhile, Moses' mother, brothers and sisters who had heard everything were singing and dancing for joy.

That night, Jonas couldn't sleep. He thought hard. Was this thing true? At one point he decided to go and ask the boys whether they hadn't stolen the money and then made up the story they had told. He went to their bedroom but changed his mind. It was past midnight and he couldn't wake them up. He returned to his bedroom, restless. "Aren't you sleeping?" his wife asked as she had noticed he couldn't stop turning himself over and over.

"How can I?" he replied.

The next morning, Jonas and his son were at Mr; Tom Scott's office two hours earlier than expected. Jonas couldn't contain his excitement. When Mr Scott arrived, he immediately recognized Moses and guessing the elderly man who accompanied the boy was his father, said to him:

"Papa, Na your son this?"

"Yes, sah," Jonas replied. "Na my son, sah. My own son, sah. My son I born for my own belly, sah."

He took them into his office and explained to Pa Jonas how he had discovered the exquisite piece of craftsmanship.

"This son intelligent plenty!" he said to Jonas.

"That is true, sah. Na my best son, sah."

At this juncture, Mr Scott counted the remaining seventy thousand francs and handed it to Moses' father.

"Thank you, sah. Thank you plenty, sah. This is too good, sah." he said effusively.

"Don't thank me, thank your son. And if he has any more such carvings, do let me know."

"Yes sah. I go tell you, sah." He then turned to his son and assured him that if ever he needed any help to produce more wooden bicycles, he should not hesitate to let him know. He kept praising Moses throughout their trek home.

Both Jonas and his wife were in high spirits. She particularly kept thanking God whom she said never slept but kept watch over those who needed him. Now hey were happy that even, if Moses did not win the scholarship, they would still be able to send him to college "by their own means." But when his results came out, not only did he pass the Common Entrance exam in the coveted List 'A' and as a result, obtained the scholarship, he also passed the First School Leaving Certificate with distinction.

2

Fateful Ride

Market day was one day we looked forward to with baited breath. And once it came, it was another eight days before the next one. This was because like in most villages in the region, our local market was held on the weekly 'country Sunday', or to put it in proper English, the weekly public holiday. This day fell once in eight days and not seven days because there are eight days in the village week. Since there are only seven in the western culture, it goes without saying that the village days on which western days fell kept changing. For instance our own public holiday was Yelighi. If you work it out you will find that if that day fell on a Sunday in one week for example, the following week it will fall on Monday, and then Tuesday, and Wednesday respectively. The market day on which the incident I am about to recount fell was a Tuesday. On that day I was one of those who left the school compound as soon as we were dismissed. It was a two-mile walk from our school to the market, yet it seemed to me that on market days I covered that in only ten minutes. So great was my desire to get to the market. You will understand why in a short while. I was told my mother was out in the market.

Once I got to the market, I hurried to the hut which my mother and some other women used as their base. So I promptly I left to look for her. I found her buying palm oil from Pa John, the Mentighi man who always surprised me with his mastery of our language, Mbelighi. Although I knew many Mentighi people who spoke other languages, Pa John was the only one I knew with such a great mastery of Mbelighi. He was a dirty old man who tied his tin of oil on his old bicycle, then rode and pushed it all the way up to Alah Mbelighi, as the village was uphill.

"Pa John, why is your oil so expensive this week?" my mother was asking.

"It's the supply mammy, it's the supply. We didn't get much oil this week. I don't know why suppliers didn't smash more of it."

"But Pa John, you always say that. You are from Mentighi where this oil is made. So how can you start telling me about supply?" My mother asked, yet looking quite pleased after dipping her finger in the large basin of oil that lay on the ground between her and Pa John, to see if it was good oil.

"No, no! That's not the point. You know I don't produce oil. I only buy and sell it. Do you think an old man like me can still have the strength to step on boiled palm kernels in order to crush them and produce oil? You know I can't do that any more. However, you know I always sell good oil."

"Yes, I know that. I have just tasted today's one. Alright, I'll take a bottle." It was only then my mother noticed I was standing next to her.

"Ah see who we have here! When did you come, son?"

"I've just arrived, mother… and I'm hungry." I said.

"Have you seen your father?"

"No, I haven't."

"You mean you haven't been to his njangis hut?"

"No, mother."

"Then go and see him." As I turned to go, she stopped me.

"Take this," she said, searching in her purse as she dug into coins and turned them around. She gave me 50 francs. I knew that as usual, I would buy takwa and kuru kuru, both of which were Hausa specialities. But first, I had to go and se my father. As soon as I entered their njangis hut, he offered me a handshake and asked: "Have you returned from school?"

"Yes, Papa." I said taking my usual standing position next to him. I knew I looked like him. So in order to excite people's curiosity, I made sure the two identical faces were next to each other. It worked because just then a man whom I hadn't seen in that hut before asked my father:

"Whose son is this?"

"Why don't you look at his face? Look at his face!"

My father handed me his horn cup which I respectfully accepted with both hands as our cultural etiquette required. I sipped the palm wine in the cup and returned it to him. He took it, used his left palm to wipe the part of the cup to which I had put my lips. Then turning back to me he inquired:

"Don't you like the wine?"

"I do, Papa. It4s only that it's too strong."

He took back his cup without any reproach and without the slightest annoyance. Then he searched his pocket and took out a one hundred franc coin which he gave me. I smiled very broadly and thanked him. That was a lot of money as far as I was concerned. Yet my joy was double, considering that my mother had already given me fifty francs. That meant I now had a hundred and fifty francs to buy enough takwa and kuru kuru to eat and be satisfied. Just then a thought crossed my mind. Why not go to my cousins' mothers' hut and look for them so that we could buy and eat together? After all, when they had money they shared their own food with me.

It turned out that only one of my cousins, Afungchwi, was around. So, together, we went in search of my two delicacies. It was I making the offer, so what he wanted did not matter. In any case, I was older than he was. Being three years his senior, I had the right to overrule him.

A few minutes later we were at the takwa and kuru kuru line. All the women and girls there knew me as I bought from them every market day. As we got nearer, they scrambled towards us with their trays and basis.

"Customer, come now! I get fine one. You no see-am?" said one.

"I beg, Papa. Look my own," said another.

"*Cus*, Na me I dey always sell for you!"

This keen competition was nothing to me. So I just ignored them and their pleas and bough from whom I preferred. We bought two takwas and two takwas, of which I gave one of each to my cousin and kept the remaining one for myself.

I could not wait to start savouring these very delicious and irresistible goodies. So at once I sank my teeth into the takwa first. This snack, as one might call it, was rounded like a ball and in fact looked like a very large lawn tennis ball. I believe groundnut paste was one of its ingredients. It was a brittle product which could come apart if pressed hard or bitten into. I loved biting into it. As I did so a chunk of it broke off and filled my mouth. Then I felt saliva in my own mouth dry up as it was absorbed by the food. I chewed and swallowed with difficulty, as the food had not been adequately mixed with saliva. Nonetheless, the taste was good and I relished it.

As Afungchwi and I enjoyed our meal, we walked around the market as was the habit, looking, examining, listening and hearing. It was now about half past four, an hour and a half since I got to the market from school. By this time the market was packed full and although there must have been over two thousand people crowded into that space that was like three quarters of a football pitch, all the different noises made in it sounded like one large continuous hum when heard from a distance.

The village market was one spot that attracted people from far and wide. People spent days on end planning for it. Some went there to sell, and others to buy. Yet others went there just to socialize. For those who wanted to meet long lost friends, it was widely known that there were two places to look in: the village market and funerals.

Here at the Muto Mbelighi, people screamed at the sight of old friends, sellers cried out to customers, buyers haggled in order to get a good bargain. Butchers picked up portions of meat, sized them up and dropped them back on the slab with disappointment. Women selling palm wine in hut bars served men coquettishly. The mean teased them.

Once Afungchwi and I finished eating, I headed towards my mother's hut and took a hut next to her as she chatted with friends. Just then, Afungchwi came running into the hut. He whispered into my ear:

"The tractor has arrived!"

"Are you sure?" I asked.

"Of course, I'm sure!"

Out I went with him, my mother taking no notice. As soon as we approached the nearby road where vehicles were packed, I spotted the tractor packed there. I also say the driver, Mr Ashangwa standing near the vehicle and conversing with someone. I became excited. At once I ran to my mother and told her I wanted to go home.

"Now?" she asked, alarmed.

"Yes, mother."

"Why?"

"I just want to go?"

"Okay; I want you to take this plastic bag with you. It has the food I am going to cook tonight and in the morning. So, you must be careful. Leave it here and let your father know you are about to go home. When you've done that, come back and collect the food bag."

I got up and walked to the door but returned to my mother. She watched me surprised. But before she could say anything, I gave her an explanation.

"I want to leave my bag here with you. "

Thereupon I sped towards my father's hut. He smiled at me as I walked in. When I told him I would like to go home, he had no objection. He did not even look surprised, unlike my mother. All he said was:

"If you are leaving now, you may as well take my umbrella with you."

"What if it rains, Papa?" I asked.

"No, it won't. You can see that outside, the sky is not dark and it has not rumbled."

As soon as I left his hut, I rushed to my mother's hut, collected the bag of foodstuffs and my school bag. After that, I looked for Afungchwi and we both made our way towards the waiting tractor.

This tractor was every little boy's dream on market days, but unfortunately not all market days. The tractor which belonged to the agricultural department's piggery section came to the market for the purchase of sweet potatoes for the pigs. Apparently, that was their staple food.

What happened was that the driver, whom we knew only as Mr Ashangwa, brought the tractor to the market, bought and loaded the pig's food single headedly. Wisely, we thought, he decided to engage us, little school boys so that we could help him with the task. So we herded around him and as soon as he had bought a bucket, head pan, basin, or basket, we scrambled over it as each one of us fought to be the one to carry it to the tractor. None of us wanted our parents to know we did this because we knew that if they did, they would give us an unforgettable beating. Fortunately, they did not catch wind of these goings-on, at least not until the incident I am recounting happened.

We were not paid for the job. Not a franc were we given in appreciation. Nevertheless, we were delighted to do it. Our only reward was that after loading all the sweet potatoes that had been bought, we would hitch a free ride home on the tractor. Even so, being granted the pleasure of jumping on the tractor was not automatic. This is because once we finished loading Mr Ashangwa would use his discretion in deciding on who would ride the tractor. If one adds to that the fact that the tractor did not come to the market until its stock of potatoes was exhausted, one can easily understand that sometimes it was weeks before some of us were made to join the chosen few.

On this day, I was chosen. Understandably, my level of excitement was high and in that moment of madness, I forgot about my brother Afungchwi whom I had instructed to stand by the tractor with my school bag, the bag of foodstuffs and my father's umbrella. When I thought about him, we had gone far into our journey. I panicked, but looking around, I found that he was also actually on the tractor. Oh, how relieved I was! My fear had been that if he was left behind, he might not remember to bring home the things I had put in his care.

We drove straight to the piggery as was the habit. Once we entered the yard and the driver reversed and parked so that the back of the tractor was directly in front of the kitchen storeroom, he ordered us:

"Get off now, boys and offload!"

Promptly, some kitchen staff brought large sacks into which we stuffed the sweet potatoes and dragged them into the storeroom. Once that was done, we started dispersing towards our various directions. Afungchwi came over to me, smiling as if very pleased with himself. We were all either smiling approvingly or talking to each other excitedly, that is, all of us who had been lucky enough to hitch a ride on the tractor on that day. As soon as I saw my cousin coming towards me, my heart missed a beat.

"Where are the things?" I screamed, alarmed.

He stopped and then asked:

"What things?"

"What things? Did you ask me what things? But the things! My school bag, the bag my mother gave me and Pa's umbrella!" Afungchwi stood there, giving me a blank look as if he had still not understood what I was talking about. As if he had just remembered, he said, "I don't know."

Oh my God! I felt like strangling him. If he had left those things somewhere back in the market, chances of ever finding them were very slim. Besides, I knew I would get three severe thrashings, one from my mother, one from my father and the third from my teacher.

Instinctively I ran to the tractor, but it was all empty. I asked Mr Ashangwa if he had seen a school bag, a plastic bag and an umbrella.

"No," he said.

I rushed into the storeroom, just in case someone had left the things there. There was no luck there either. Now I felt I had no chance than to rush back to the market, which was, believe it or not, two miles away. I ran like a mad man. Although I knew that when I started, Afungchwi was already running after me, by the time I got to the market out of breath, I had lost him. I suppose that as I was older and stronger, I outran him. I was thirteen and he, ten.

By now there were very few people left in the market. I looked where the tractor had stood but could not find the things I was looking for. Deeply worried, I rushed around the market, just looking anywhere, but still did not find them. Although there was a chance one of my parents could have found them and taken them into their hut, I did not have the courage to go and ask them. In any case, they were unlikely to be still in the market. Most of the huts had been locked up already and there were only a few people left in the market. These were busy packing up.

14

After wondering what I could do, I decided to go home. I planned a strategy which I would execute once I got near our compound. It was that as soon as I got there I would start crying. I did so. Tears poured down my eyes and I was saying:

"What shall I do? Where is Pap? Where is Mama?"

Having heard me, my parents who had identified my distraught voice, rushed out very concerned.

"What's it? What's the matter?" my father inquired.

"I think he has misplaced the things he was supposed to bring home. Don't you see he hasn't got them?" came my mother's instinctive reaction.

"It's not me, Papa. It's Afungchwi. I gave them to him."

"You did what?" My father thundered, grabbing me by the hand. I knew what would happen next. However, I was surprised that contrary to all expectations, and this for reasons far beyond my comprehension as it had never happened before, my father suddenly let go of my hand and simply said:

"Listen, little son. You are lucky I and not in a bad mood today. Otherwise, I would beat the hell out of you. How could you have been so careless?"

"I don't know, Papa. I'm sorry. I'm sorry." I replied, crying even louder.

My father walked into the house and my mother said:

"It's alright, son. It's alright."

She then took me into the house and we had our evening meal. None of my brothers or sisters reproached me. I suppose they believe it was not my fault. The following morning before I left for school, my father asked me to stop at Pa Nibalum's store and collect items to replace the ones I had lost in my school bag. He warned me that if this kind of carelessness repeated itself, I would have to pay for it 'through the nose'. I was thankful. To me what my parents had just done and the manner in which they did it was really nothing short of a miracle.

15

Nevertheless, at school, I was not out of the woods yet. Firstly I was faced with the Herculean task of copying notes and drawing maps and diagrams in the new exercise books I had bought. I could not ask friends to help because if my teachers found that out, I would be in trouble.

Just as I has expected, my teacher Mr Cosmas sound found that I had lost my books. He did so the very day I took my new books to school. While he was giving us a mental arithmetic test, he passed near my book and noticed I was writing in a new book. But Contrary to what I expected, he did not say anything about the book. But later when we had Nature Study and he asked us to bring our books up to his table, he noticed that again, I had a new book.

"Come back here, Etta Charles!" he said. My heart sank.

"How many new books are you starting today?" I hesitated, dumbfounded.

"Bring me all your books!" he ordered.

I went to my desk, picked up the plastic bag that now served as my school bag, dug my hand into it while the teacher watched me intently, and took out some books.

"I mean all! Bring me all the books!" Mr Cosmas shouted.

Left with no choice, I removed all the books and went up to him.

"No, can you tell me what is going on?"

"I… I lost my bag yesterday, sir."

"I see. And you thought you could get away with it?"

"No sir. I… I…"

"Just don't bother!" he warned. "Where is my cane?" he said, looking around.

"Turn round!" he commanded.

I did and he gave me twenty loud and painful solid strokes of the cane. After that he ordered me to return to my seat, warning:

"If you are so careless again, I will make it forty eight, not just twenty four. And by the way there is something which you children don't seem to understand. Here at Saint Francis' School, we are not just teaching you. We are also training you to be good, careful and responsible catholic children."

When I went home that day, I told my mother what had happened at school. Her reply was:

"Your teacher was right in what he did. I also hope that you will not be so careless next time."

3

One Way Ticket

The news spread like wild fire in the village. At long last after twenty years in Britain without a single visit back home, she was coming back. People debated about what she would look like. Some wondered what things she would bring back from the white man's country. Yet others speculated about what she would give them personally. Whatever was the case, she was the talk of the village.

When Ma Emilia left Cameroon, it was to study secretarial duties at the Oxford College of Applied Languages In London on a Cameroon Government Scholarship. After she finished the course, she decided to stay on and train as a nurse. This was because she had heard that even while a student nurse, she would be paid a monthly allowance that was handsome. When the training which lasted some three years was over, she was immediately offered a job in one of the London hospitals. Although it was well known that trained nurses were easily employed, Ma Emilia learned when she started the course that psychiatric nurses were more in demand than their counterparts in the geriatric, paediatric and community fields. So she chose psychiatric nursing as her area of specialisation in the second and final years. In the end it was clear that she had made the right choice, for as soon as her batch graduated, those of them who were psychiatric nurses were actually offered jobs without applying for them.

Ma Emilia enjoyed her job very much. She was a very friendly and jovial nurse, well liked by colleagues and patients. Since her patients were mentally handicapped, or 'had learning difficulties', as British authorities preferred to put it, they often behaved abnormally. Sometimes, one of them would leave his bed, get out of the ward and start making about aimlessly. Once one was found chewing part of his bed linen which he claimed was a loaf of bread. Another left his bed and joined a co-patient in his own bed, claiming the latter was his wife, although that spouse had died five years previously. Ma Emilia had a tactful way with these patients. She would put her hand round them and say: "Come on darling, I know you need love. I can assure you that we love you here." It worked like magic each time she used it.

After working for a few months, Ma Emilia moved out of the council flat that she was sharing with a Nigerian friend, Dorothy, and took up residence in her own council flat. It was a two bedroom flat which she did up gradually, wall paper, furniture, gas and electricity. Later on, she installed a phone in it. Six months after she started work, she got a boyfriend, one who became so serious afterwards that they got married. His name was Peter and he too, like Dorothy, was from Nigeria. In fact, he and Dorothy were cousins. It was through Dorothy that Ma Emilia met him. The two cousins were Igbos from Umuahia. After Peter and Ma Emilia had seen each other for six months, Peter moved into Ma Emilia's flat. A year later, they had a son whom they named Edward. Two years later they had another son whom they named James. He was followed by a daughter, Patricia.

Ma Emilia communicated regularly with the family back home in her first year in Britain. She wrote back to her parents back in the village, her brothers and sisters in Kumba, Douala and Bamenda every month, even when she did not get replies. In the second year she started failing to answer some letters and the replies she wrote were terse and hasty. She would write to close friends and relatives only once in a quarter, if at all. After that, she only wrote about twice a year. By the time she got into her fourth year, she stopped writing altogether. Floods of letters came from home, none of which was answered. Her family and friends became worried. Whenever her parents heard that a child of the village was visiting from Britain, they would search for the child and ask:

"Did you ever see this Emilia at all?"

Before the interlocutor could reply, they would continue: "How can a child just disappear like that?"

Her mother, in tears would say:

"I have heard that she has been seen. If she doesn't want to write to us as she used to do, why doesn't she just tell someone to let us know she is in good health?"

Ten years passed since Ma Emilia left the country. It was now six years since she was last heard from. Back at home, the family talked and worried about her less and less. Some concluded she was dead.

However, the breakthrough came about on a certain Sunday when her parents were attending service at the village Presbyterian Church. As the week's newly arrived letters were read out in church at the end of worship, Ma Emilia's father heard his name called among those who were recipients of letters that had arrived care of the church's post box. As was the practice, the letter was handed to him. But since he did not know how to read, having never been to school, he just put it and his pocket and took no further notice of it. It did not occur to him at all or anyone else in that church on that day that the letter could be from his long lost daughter in Europe. Not even Ma Emilia's mother or the pastor who distributed the mails suspected anything of that kind. Anyway, perhaps on the part of the pastor, it was negligence more than anything else. He had quite q sizeable chunk of mails to read out that week. Consequently, he was rushing through them, especially as the sermon had been quite long and the day's announcements were yet to come. Despite the lack of expectation, the letter turned out to be from Ma Emilia. In it she apologized for her long silence which she attributed to grave difficulties which had made it necessary for her to go out of circulation and sort out her life.

The most interesting part of the letter was a photograph she sent of herself, her husband, their two boys and the girl. To crown it all, she said she would be coming home the following month to show the family her children. Unfortunately she said Peter could not come because he was at work and it was not possible for her vacation period to coincide with his. This letter, as it turned out, had been read before the congregation dispersed because as soon as they rose, Ma Emilia went over to her husband and said:

"Nei Fang Mbeng. Who sent you a letter?"

"I don't know," he said absent minded.

"But then, give it to someone to look at." As she spoke she grabbed someone by the arm:

"John, why are you a teacher. Come and read this letter for Nei Fang Mbeng." Just like her husband, Mami Azi Arimboh had not been to school. So she too could not read.

As soon as John the teacher looked at the envelope and saw the name of the sender, he screamed. That reaction drew a lot of attention from those present as they all turned in the direction of the teacher.

"Is someone dead, John?" Ma Emilia's mother inquired, alarmed.

"Dead, Mami? No! It's life. Life, not death. This letter is from your daughter in the white man's country. It's from Emilia!"

"From whom? Emilia? Which Emilia? Did she …"

"What did he say, Josepha?"? Ma Emilia's father asked his wife, as he came closer to her and John the teacher.

Husband and wife were soon to understand that they were not dreaming. It was true that their runaway daughter had broken the ice.

As this was a village affair and a matter that broke out during a social event that brought much of the village together, everyone was in a joyous mood. They sang and danced in the church yard. Some people in compounds nearby joined in the merry making. The pastor, like the true man of God he was, invited everyone back into the church so that they could pray for the "prodigal daughter."

That evening Nei Fan Mbeng and his Wife Ma wife Ma Azi Arimboh reflected on the contents of their daughter's letter. Firstly, they were very happy that she was alive and had broken the silence. They were very pleased she had settled down, got married and 'given' them grand children among whom her father noted there was a boy. However, they still felt that there were several unanswered questions about their daughter. How, for instance, could Emilia say she was married when the family back home had not heard about it before it happened? Who made marriage arrangements? According to tradition, any man wanting to get married to her should have started by asking his own father to make contact with him, Ma Emilia's father, who would then direct him to her uncles and aunts. As far as they knew, this had not happened. So how could she talk of marriage? And this boy, Peter, what village did he come from? Was he a 'country boy', which actually meant, 'a boy from her own tribe'? What kind of work was this that stopped him from coming to reveal himself to them? Nevertheless, based on what they could see in the photographs Emilia sent, they were happy that their daughter had not got marries to a white man. They recalled Pa Ngam's son who had also studied in Britain but returned with a white wife. Ma Emilia's father had one question he always asked:

"Why does anyone ever go and choose a woman who can't pound ones *achoo* for one to enjoy totally?"

Despite The high level of their concerns, what they did not know was that, not only was Ma Emilia's husband not from the village, he was not even from Cameroon.

While the family in Cameroon was waiting for their believed daughter back in Britain, she too was greatly looking forward to the trip. Peter who was a nice guy helped her a great deal to prepare for the trip. He gave her money to buy things to carry along to the family. He bought some personally. Although he had never met any member of his wife's family, he knew a lot about them, having made all kinds of inquiries from his wife. So before she left, he wrote letters to in-laws he had only heard about. To say the truth, Ma Emilia was quite happy with her husband. When he started courting her, her friends, including her best friend Priscilla, who was also a nurse, and a paediatric nurse at that, tried to talk her out of it. Their bone of contention was that Nigerians were too idealistic to date the down-to-earth Cameroonians. They argued that Nigerians were too extravagant. They did everything in double sizes and were unreliable. When she asked them what they meant by 'extravagant', they replied that it meant Nigerians were rogues and crooks. She brushed aside the criticisms on the grounds that there was no way all Nigerians could be so bad, just as not all Cameroonian men could be good. So she braved all the odds, dated Peter and got married to him. She had since not regretted it because Peter had turned each and every one of those arguments on its head. In short, she found Peter to be a very good husband.

***

The day Ma Emilia got to the village, everyone came out. There was singing and dancing in her father's compound. Even the Fon sent a goodwill message. Her children, especially the older ones, Edward and James who were now aged five and three respectively, were shocked, frightened and curious about the way of life in the village. For the first time, they saw live hens and cocks grazing freely in the open. Edward made it a point to chase them each time he saw any of them passing by. At first the two children refused to use pit toilets because they looked awful, with their sweating mouths and maggot-infested bellies. It made them want to throw up. However, they soon adapted and the longer they stayed, the more they got accustomed to things. By the time they had been in the country for the one month they had budgeted, they had on the whole also started adapting to the general African way of life. It was only their accent that remained stoically British. Interestingly, their mother found it harder to adapt. She was very choosy about the food she ate, used her own drugs when she was ill and only drank mineral water. Little Patricia was too young to know what was going on. She did not seem to know she was in a different country. She was only four months old.

After some time, Ma Emilia left the village to spend some time with family members and friends in the towns. While she was at the home of one of her uncle's, in fact, the direct junior brother of her father, the former called one of his daughters.

"Emilia, my daughter!" her uncle Nei Ndi called out.

"Yes, Papa," replied Ma Emilia who despite her difficulties in adaptation, had not completely forgotten custom and tradition.

"This young girl you see here is your sister;"

"What is her name, Papa?"

"Lum. Anatacha Lum," said Nei Ndi. The name was actually Anastasia.

"How are you, Lum" Ma Emilia asked, trying to sound very traditional.

"Fine, Auntie;"

"How old are you?

"I am 15."

"Do you go to college?"

"No, Auntie. I've finished. I've just completed from Mandzah Government Secondary School."

"You mean you have your 'O' Levels?

"Yes, Auntie."

"In how many subjects?"

"Eight, Auntie. Eight including maths and English."

"That's very good. What do you want to do now?"

At that point Anastasia's father stepped in.

"That's why I called her so that you could see her, my daughter."

"I don't understand, Papa. What do you mean?"

"I have come to give you Anatacha."

"Give her to me, Papa?"

"Yes. Give her to you to take to the white man's country."

"Why, Papa? What's the reason for that?"

"So that she can help you with house work. Let her just stay in the house with you and help. I know you have three children, with the last one being less than a year old. I am sure you need help with them."

"Yes, I need help, Papa. But how do you uproot a young girl from her studies and send her to work for someone? How about her education?"

"You are not someone, my daughter. You are my daughter and her sister. What is the point of her going to school if she can't help you in need? As for her education, will she not be learning how to live in the white man's country when she is with you? Is that not education?"

"Okay, Papa. I have heard and understood you. But let me think about it. Let me sleep on it."

Later that day, Ma Emilia discussed the offer with her own parents. They both agreed that there was nothing wrong with her taking Anastasia to help her in Britain. So she made contact with the British embassy in Yaounde. This was before Cameroon joined the Commonwealth and the British Embassy in Cameroon became the 'British High Commission', just as the Cameroon Embassy in Britain became the 'Cameroon High Commission'.

By the time Ma Emilia left the village, the High Commission had granted Anastasia's visa. There was another feast for this long lost daughter who was about to return to the land from whence she had come with so much to her credit. Elder after elder of the village rose and showered blessings on her. The elder who rubbed cam wood on her forehead and those of her children including Anastasia, affirmed that the ancestors would carry them safely to their destination. Nevertheless, one refrain was heard repeatedly as the elders spoke. This was that they also wanted to see Ma Emilia's husband.

"He has to come and see us about you. He can't continue to leave things hanging. This unsettled state of affairs is not good for you or the children, but especially for the children. If the spirits are angry with us, it is you people who will be affected. Your husband must really hurry and rectify things" they insisted.

Everyone thanked Ma Emilia for the presents she had brought. Those who had not been lucky to receive one asked her not to forget them next time. Those who got presents said she had done well by thinking about them. Even so, they said they wanted more the next time she was coming home. Some people, especially her mother, wept as she left. Ma Emilia also wept when she saw her mother weeping.

"Mother, I must go. Don't worry, I will write often.'"

"Thank you my daughter. I don't know whether the next time you are coming back, you will still find your father and me alive. You know we are old and sickly and tired."

"No, mother; Nothing will happen to you. I'm sure you will still be here. I'll try and see if I can come here next year and every year after that. The only problem is the cost. It's very expensive.'

'Don't worry my daughter. Go well! May the good God take you back safely?"

***

When Ma Emilia returned to Britain, her husband, true to himself, was very pleased that a relative from home had come to help them. He personally wrote to Ma Emilia's parents and Nei Ndi to thank them for the hospitality they gave his wife and children. He said he was particularly impressed that they had found someone to come and assist them with looking after the children.

Ma Emilia, Peter and children found Anastasia to be great fun. She did her work diligently. It took her only a few months to be able to find her way around. She was now able to go to the major places alone. These included the play school and nursery school where James and Edward went, the doctor's surgery, the town's supermarkets, church and local library. On week days when the children went to school and their parents to work, Anastasia stayed at home with Patricia who was still too small to go anywhere by herself. She knew when to feed the baby, when to put her to bed and when to take her for a walk.

After Anastasia had been with the Chukwumas for six months approximately, Ma Emilia and her husband decided that because the girl was so good, when Patricia was two years old, Anastasia would be enrolled in a college in London for part time evening studies so that she could do her 'A' Levels. That would be a drastic change in orientation because going to school had not been the reason why Anastasia was sent to London by her father.

When the time came, Anastasia joined Norburington Community College where she attended school only two days a week. Consequently, she was able to continue helping at home, especially with Little Patricia. Anastasia's course progressed quite well. She and Ma Emilia wrote home to let everyone know that she had been made to return to school in order to obtain her Advanced Levels. Ma Emilia's father wrote back to thank his daughter for holding her junior sister's hand in the march towards a brighter and better future. He told her that was how it should be.

"My Dear daughter, what you and your husband have done for your junior sister, Anastasia, is very significant and praiseworthy because it shows that you aren't only thinking of yourselves."

Anastasia's own father did not write. Ma Emilia did not think anything about it. She only did when things turned sour as we shall soon learn.

When 'A' Level results came out, Anastasia passed. Ma Emilia and Peter decided that the best thing for her to do was to train as a nurse because that would enable her to earn while learning and thereafter, be sure of a job after training. Anastasia agreed. Once in a while and with the blessings of her 'elder' sister, Anastasia would send some money home to her parents and some to her uncle and wife. Nevertheless, she was still a student, being paid only a small allowance for the purchase of course books and incidentals. That was why Ma Emilia took the pains in joining Anastasia to explain to the people back home that it was not a salary that latter was earning.

When she finished her course and started working she sent a reasonable sum of money home from her salary. She with the benediction of Ma Emilia, decided to use the salary for the next few months, finding her a place of her own to live, equipping it and helping her to move into it. Within four months, she had mobbed into the flat which was located in another housing estate, not far from Ma Emilia's own. Not long after that, Ma Emilia and her family moved into a house they had just bought in the Golders Green area of North London. Even so, the two cousins kept in touch with each other.

Some months later, Ma Emilia received a bombshell from Anastasia's father. It was a shocking and most annoying letter which had been totally unexpected and as Ma Emilia felt, completely uncalled for. The section of it that might interest you the reader most, is:

"Ever since my daughter started working, you have been chopping her money. We are dying here of poverty. We don't have money to buy salt or oil or medicines. Yet we are sick and hungry all the time. So I want you to send my daughter back to me instead of using and exploiting her like you are doing."

Revolted by the letter which she discussed with her husband, Ma Emilia picked up the telephone and rang Anastasia. Both of them had telephones at home. That point is very important because at the time fixed phones were the only means by which people could have immediate contact with each other. It was only later that mobile cordless telephones arrived on the communication scene and became the order of the day. Today as we all know, everyone has them, even children. One can not help wondering what other new communication gadget modern technology is planning to spring on the unsuspecting consumer.

When Ma Emilia explained to her cousin what had just happened, Anastasia felt equally hurt. Within forty five minutes, she was at Ma Emilia's place. If she had her way, she would have flown to her 'sister's flat, instead of walking and catching the tube. So great was her anxiety and anguish! But alas, the fastest way of getting there was only the underground. When Anastasia read the letter, she found it hard to believe that her father could have sent it to Ma Emilia of all people. After all, her cousin was the one who had made her what she was today.

She assured Ma Emilia that as soon as she got back to her flat, she would write to her father. She did, and she told him exactly what she thought. But when her Old Man replied a month later, he simply reiterated what he had said in the previous letter to Ma Emilia. He twisted the knife further by adding that he was very ill and was not sure he would survive. To conclude, he said: "So, pack your bags and come back home!"

At the same time, he wrote again to Anastasia's cousin, saying he wanted his daughter back. He accused Ma Emilia of having collected her from home only to go to London and confiscate her salary and then enslave her. The two cousins decided that it since it was becoming too much, the best thing would be for Anastasia to return to her father in Cameroon. It was important for her to see her sick father before he died, if it came to that.

When Anastasia got to Cameroon, she found, much to her consternation that although her father looked older and frailer than he was at the time she left for Britain, there did not seem to be anything wrong with him. The story of him being very sick and therefore close to death was therefore simply an invention of his own.

"Papa, what is the problem with your health?" she asked.

"Oh, do I even know, my daughter? I am an old man and all parts of my body are old. I am just feeling pains all over. General body pains. Pains here, pains there; pains everywhere."

"But you don't look as bad as you said you were!"

"Oh! What do you know, my daughter? Can you ever tell what is going on in an old man's body just by looking at his appearance? And in any case, if you feel I am not ill enough, who knows when that kind of serious illness may strike?"

Anastasia then decided to let sleeping dogs lie. In the few days that followed, she helped her mother with the house work. She went to the farm with her, and answered questions about the white man's land from the many villages that came to see her. One evening in her mother's kitchen, she asked her mother:

"Mother, did you know about this letter Papa wrote to Ma Emilia, saying he wanted her to send me back to him because she was taking my money?"

"Yes, he told me about it. In fact, he had complained very often about your sister taking your money from you."

"But mother, I can't stay. I've got my job to go back to."

"Don't worry then. We'll have to try and reason with him, some how or other."

The following day, Anastasia's father sent for her.

"Yes, Papa!"

"Sit down, my daughter. Did you hear what I said in my letter about wanting you to return home?"

"Yes, Papa. But I don't understand why you wanted me to return home."

"I don't think your big sister has been treating you well. She has been using your money."

"Who told you that, Papa? How is Ma Emilia using my money?"

"If she is not using it, then where has it been going? You don't send us money every month. So where has it been going?;

"But how can you say that, Papa? I've just moved into my own place, which means I now pay rents. I had to equip the place too. I now buy my own food and son on."

"Yes; But that doesn't mean you should forget us here."

"But I haven't forgotten you, father. I send you money when I can."

"When you can? How about when you can't? What do we do then? Do we die?"

"How can you die, Papa?"

"In any case, I want you to stay here in Cameroon."

"Then, how about my job?"

"You can look for a job here in Cameroon. "

"But, Papa…"

"There is no but. Since when did you start arguing with me? Is that what you have learned where you went? What I am saying is that I don't want you to stay in a foreign land where you have no one to advise you on what to do with your money. Before you realise it you'll have nothing left."

"But Papa, how can you talk like that? There is Ma Emilia to advise me when I need advice. Besides, I'm not a baby."

"There may be Ma Emilia to advise you as you say. But what if she doesn't and it turns out that you feel you don't need advice, whereas the fact is that unknown to you, you do need it badly? And talking about yourself, remember that you may be working now and earning money, but the truth is that you are still a baby. Shoulders can never be higher than the head. And regarding this constant talk about Emilia, if she is not taking the money from you already, who knows? She may do so later. These are the reasons why I think you should stay here in Cameroon instead of going back to England."

"But Papa, what about my job?"

"You can find another job here. I told you so. After all you trained in the white man's country. You didn't train locally like most of these people here. So, you are worth gold here in Cameroon. So how can you doubt that you'll have a job here?"

From that day, Pa Ndi did everything possible to sow the seeds of misgiving and misapprehension in the mind of his daughter. He dampened her spirits about returning to Britain and since Anastasia was the kind of child who would not disobey her parents, especially her father, she stayed on in Cameroon. But inwardly, she was perturbed because this dramatic change in circumstances was really not to her taste.

Month after month came and went. In the meantime, the pinch was not yet being felt fully because Anastasia still had some money on her. As a result, her abortive attempts at finding a job locally were not too forcefully felt either. Then one day she told her parents she was going to Yaounde, the national capital to see if she could be employed as a nurse at the General Hospital.

"That's good, my daughter. Go well. You have my blessings."

When Anastasia got to Yaounde, a city she had not visited before, she lived in the house of a son of her own village, a married man with children, who worked in the ministry of National Education. It was a small house, which meant that her arrival made the already crowded place even more crowded. Nonetheless, her hosts had enough foresight to know that if she succeeded in her job search, she might give them or the children some help, some day, somehow. So they tolerated her. Anastasia's task consisted first of all of obtaining confirmation from the ministry of Public Health that there was a job vacancy for her at the hospital. Next, there was a lot of paper work to push around. When her employment was confirmed, she would have to go to the Ministry of Public Service for integration as a civil servant. After that she would go to the Ministry of Finance to see to it that her salary was set up. In a world where things work well and people do their job diligently, the entire process could have taken only a week. But then, as Anastasia would find out, much to her own detriment, six months later, she was still at the starting block. People responded slowly, some did not respond at all, others told her blatant lies and most demanded money illegally before even looking at her file.

Soon, the little money Anastasia had taken to Yaounde got finished. Her hosts borrowed from friends so that she could continue the task she had begun. In less than a month, that money was finished too. At this point, she had no choice than to return to her parents in the village. By this time her return ticket to London had expired, so had the date on which she was expected to resume work at the hospital. She did not have enough money to call her bosses back in London and even invent some justifications for what was going on. In the mean time, they the bosses wondered what the matter was. Could Anastasia have abandoned her job and returned to her country in Africa without letting them know? Before long, they started making arrangements to replace her because they felt that although she had been a very nice person while she was with them, they also had to render compelling accounts to their own bosses and convincingly explain the absence to inquiring patients. Ma Emilia and Peter, who had also not heard a single word from Anastasia, feared something drastic must have happened to her. They wrote home to find out but received no replies.

When the now traumatized Anastasia returned to the village and narrated the bitter experiences she had in the national capital, she went further and told them that she had run out of money. So, could they borrow some from somewhere so that she could return to the capital and continue her job search?

"Money from us, my daughter? But we are poor, old people who have nothing. Where do you expect us to get money from?"

"But Papa, can't you borrow from someone? Surely, you know people around here!"

"Borrow from whom? Does anybody in the village have money to lend? Do you know any such person?" And so it was, Anastasia's fate was sealed.

One month passed, two months passed, three months passed, and the poor girl had got nowhere. She became very worried and depressed and cried a lot. Not long afterwards, she was taken ill. It seemed that she had malaria. In the mad rush to return to Cameroon from Britain, she had not remembered to take her anti-malarial tablets. It was clear that since she had lived out of Africa, a mosquito infested zone, for so long, her body's natural resistance to malaria had weakened and collapsed. Anastasia took some tablets that were at home but she did not get well. Then she tried the Village Health Centre, but still saw no improvement in her situation. A week later, she was getting worse. Finally, seeing that they might lose her, villagers contributed money and she was transported to the General Hospital. Unfortunately, her arrival at the hospital was too little, too late. She died the following day.

4

One of a Kind

It was the very start of the school year and on this first day of the term children could be seen hurrying to their different schools. There were three in Banakuf Village, of which St. John's Primary School was the largest. The other two included one run by the Presbyterians and the third, by the State. Like other State primary schools, the latter was officially named, 'Government Primary School' Banakuf.

St John's which was a Catholic school was the most prominent of the three. It was the oldest, the most widely known and the one which had made its mark in many ways among schools in the Parish catchment's area. St. John's excelled in sports and athletics, and also led the way in terms of cultural manifestations such as traditional dances. Whenever the school's team was playing, locals from whatever village they were playing in would turn out massively and not only watch but also cheer it on. Nonetheless, on such occasions when the match was not being played in Banakuf, there would be some hostility from some of the hosts. Some spectators would shout out: "Go away! We don't want you here!" Usually, Banakuf players would ignore the taunts and just play on. While St. John's boys and girls staged the school's traditional dance– the "Mandere," which was a lively, colourful and skilful display of dance, music and traditional regalia, some onlookers would join in. Those who could not for want of space would stay where they were and execute the dance in their own way.

As St. John's was located in the very heart of the village, its pupils came from the north, south, east and west. The Presbyterian school was located in the south-east, and the Government School in the North-West. While the former was situated near the border with Banakuf's southerly neighbour Balangu, the Government School was in the urbanized part of the village. Unfortunately, it only went up to Class Four, while the two mission schools had the terminal Class Seven. As a result, children who finished Class Four at the Government School were then made to choose to continue their studies at one of the two mission schools.

On this first day of the term, some of the children who trekked to school from the urbanized district of Banakuf called Nteh Mbang soon noticed that this was a first day of the term with a difference. That evening, one pupil, Martin Mbeto who was in Class Seven and kept a diary, noted in his book of the records:

"I will never forget today. Who is this new teacher? As soon as my friends and I saw him walking to school this morning with Mr. Anong, Mr. Lukong and Miss Ngwang, we knew he must be a new teacher.

But he was so different from all of our teachers. He is by far the most stout, the tallest, the most handsome and the most friendly. The English he speaks is very different. His pronunciation is like that of an African who has lived in England, like the English spoken by white fathers. Maybe he has lived there. When my friends and I saw this new teacher, we started hoping that he would be our teacher. However, when we got to school, we discovered he is a Class Six teacher, not a Class 7 one. As a result, I don't know his name.

Nobody asked Mr John Javizhi where he came from. No pupil did, and no teacher did. People were happy to have dealings with him where he was, that is, in the present. His past was therefore not an issue. Nonetheless, perhaps it was because this was the way teachers and consequently their pupils, behaved at this school. As a matter of fact, Mr. Javizhi was not the only teacher who was not asked where he and been before coming to Banakuf, at least, not on the first day. However, being the good teacher and communicator he was, he introduced himself to his interlocutors before they even had time to wonder about where he came from any further.

It was therefore not surprising that when he met his (class 6B) for the first time, he started by introducing himself:

"Good morning, boys and girls," he said, pausing for them to respond.

"My name is John C. Javizhi and I am your new teacher. Do you understand me? Before coming here I was an English teacher at St. Mark's Secondary School in Kundu. By transferring me to this primary school, the manager must have thought he was punishing me. But far from it, I see my stint here as a challenge I relish. I must confess that so far, I like what I have seen of the school. I think you are a nice bunch of pupils and I hope you won't disappoint me. I believe in hard work. Some hard work with prayer and optimism – call it faith, if you like, always pays. Any questions?

"Yes, Sir!" said one boy as he raised his hand.

"Yes, young man. What is your name?"

"Buluh, Sir"

"And is that your first name or your surname?"

"Pardon, Sir?"

"Are you saying 'pardon' because you didn't hear me well or because you heard but you didn't understand? Quiet, the rest of you! I don't tolerate noise when I 'm talking or listening to someone. When you talk at the same time, you distract me and make me strain my ears unnecessarily."

Turning to the boy who spoke first, the teacher said:

"You said you are Buluh. Is that your own name by which people call you or your father's name which you must have taken just as people bear their fathers' names, and wives their husbands' names?"

39

"It's my father's name, Sir."

"Then, that's your surname. What's your other name?"

"Francis, Sir."

"Then that's your first name. Are you a Christian?"

"No, Sir. I am a catholic."

"If you are a catholic, then you are a Christian. The word simply means, 'follower of Christ'. Your first name can also be your Christian name. What was your question, Francis?"

"Please, Sir. If you were teaching at St. Mark's as you say, then how manage did you leave such a higher school for a primary school like this one?"

"First of all, Francis, you have used a grammatically wrong expression which must be corrected. The phrase, 'how manage did you' is not English. What should Francis have said, class? Yes, the young lady there!"

"He should have said: "Why did you?" said Gladys Eta, one of the brightest in the class. Francis was the boldest.

"That's right! He could also have said, 'how was it that…?'."

Turning to Francis, Mr Javizhi said: "Well, I left St. Mark's because of a misunderstanding between the principal and me. That's all. Any more questions? Yes, that young lady who spoke a while ago."

"Please Sir, my name is Gladys Eta and I wish to know why you use so many big words."

"Big words, like which one?"

"Please sir, you said 'utmitistic', for example."

The teacher laughed: "The longer we stay and work with each other, the more you will understand that the words I use are not as strange as you think. And by the way, the word was 'optimistic', not 'utmitistic' as you thought. It means, 'being hopeful of the future."

Having said that, Mr. Javizhi asked one of the pupils to clean the board. As he was doing so, the teacher announced to the class: "Well, our next lesson is arithmetic. I would like you to take out your arithmetic books. We are going to tackle simple interest today."

***

Mr. Javizhi did things differently, and it did not take long before the teachers began to notice this. For instance, although he had a cane, unlike the other teachers, he never used it to beat children. His was used exclusively to point to texts on the board. Once asked by a colleague why he never caned pupils, Mr. Javizhi replied: "I doubt that it works in terms of yielding the desired result. I believe in scolding children when they do something wrong. I ask them pointed questions and get them to reason with me. They must be made to understand and believe in what they do. The cane simply forces them to do things. In the end they are more rebellious than cooperative." Despite this line of action, Mr. Javizhi was authoritative and respected.

One day, during the long break, Mr Javizhi strolled towards his nearest neighbour, the Class 6A teacher, Mr. James Noba:

"Are you there? Are you there, Mr. Noba?"

"Yes, Mr. Javizhi."

"I was just wondering. What do you do here during long break, like now?"

"Well, it depends on the individual, doesn't it? Some teachers stay in their classrooms and eat their lunch or correct books. Others join colleagues for chats. There are of course, those who may be on duty."

"You mean you don't do sports?"

"Oh no! Who would play football at this time of the day?"

"No, I didn't mean football. I was thinking of volleyball. We started this at my old school and before long, it was a top hit with teachers queuing to have a go. Even children left their own pastimes and enjoyed it from the sidelines."

"It sounds like a good idea. Why don't you discuss it with the sports master?"

41

"I will, certainly. But who is the sports master?"

"There he is! Over there, watching those boys over there, near the school garden, amusing themselves with a football."

As soon as Mr. Javizhi spoke to the sports master, the latter went to see the headmaster who approved the application and authorized the disbursement of some funds. Within a fortnight, a site had been found and a volleyball pitch constructed. The very minute construction work ended, a match took place between two groups of teachers, with Mr. Javizhi being the organiser and coach.

Thereafter a game of volleyball between teachers at lunchtime became a ritual. Pupils stood at the touchline and watched. Parents setting off for some business stopped by for some time and watched before moving on. This happened all the time as the main road to the village (it ended at the Fon's palace) actually cut through the school compound, dividing it into two nearly equal parts. The volleyball pitch was on the left side of the compound, quite close to the road, as one faced the palace direction. Supposing a serious passer-by decided to ignore the match and just walk past, this pretence would only last for a few seconds as the shouts, screams; yells and whistling of players were loud enough to distract the most focused of people.

It was great fun to watch Mr. Javizhi play volleyball. He was by far the best player. There was no doubt tat his great height and generous build made him an ideal player. In fact, his height earned him the nickname of 'International Height', from us pupils. However, the pupils also called him by other names such as 'Mr. Perfect' not intended to be pejorative.

Mr Javizhi was the neatest teacher in the school. He was always clean, dressed well and spoke well, not only in his choice of language but also in his avoidance of insults and humiliating words such as 'fool', 'idiot', 'thief' and 'liar' when speaking to or referring to pupils.

The girls found him to be the most handsome of the male teachers. In fact, one girl, then in Class 7, recalled to her friends that in all her six years at St. John's there had not been a teacher as handsome as Mr. Javizhi. In their own little groups of friends, pupils often wondered what life was like in Mr. Javizhi's home. "His children must be very happy," said one boy. However, what the boy did not know was that Mr Javizhi was not a father, neither was he even married. He was going to get married while at St. John's. But we will come to that later.

Back on the volleyball pitch, Mr. Javizhi was in his element. He would exclaim "Ooh!" as he hit the ball. When he was serving he held the ball in his left hand, rolled it with his fingers , and then standing with his left foot forward, he hit the ball high up in the sky. As it came down accelerating with the force of gravity, he struck it and it shot over the net onto the opposing side. None of his opponents ever liked receiving his volleys because as soon as they made contact with it, the ball got deflected out of the court. Then that would earn a point for the server's side. And then Mr. Javizhi would have to serve again and inflict more loss of points on the other side.

"Mr. Javizhi, your shots are poisoned!" Mr. Ndasi would exclaim.

"You haven't seen anything yet, Mr. Ndasi" came the reply. But if there were no pupils around, the two teachers would call each other by first names.

Mr. Javizhi opponents were in deeper trouble when he was at the net. His team mates knew this only too well and so always passed him the ball so that he could deliver the finishing stroke. Whenever he was doing this, Mr. Javizhi would leap in the air, and helped by his height, slam the ball into the opposing court as he cried "Ooh!" If the slam was successfully executed, then he beamed from ear to ear and turning to his team mates, he would say "Did you see that?" Such moments were very frequent when Mr. Javizhi played.

He was so good at the net that whenever his opponents saw him leaping with his hand raised, they ran away instead of positioning themselves to receive the ball. Dull moments descended upon the volleyball pitch when for some reason Mr. Javizhi was away from school. Often, on such days there were no volleyball matches. To Mr. Javizhi's credit, a school volleyball team for pupils was formed within months of his arrival at St. John's. By this time no other school in the parish had a volleyball team. Within a year, each school had one. Inter-school volleyball competitions were held with St. John's winning the trophy until Mr. Javizhi's departure from the school.

Despite Mr Javizhi's excellence, he was far from being a perfect man. Firstly, he was not a good singer and so while other teachers would, once in a while, teach a song here and there, Mr Javizhi never taught any. Whenever he was present at singing lessons, he would stand and watch, more for the sake of being there just in case the children were "up to something," than for the purpose of singing. At such times he would single out a pupil, or stop the teacher teaching and say something like: "Come on children! You can't sing properly without opening your mouths. Open them and enunciate the words! Sorry for interrupting, my dear colleague."

The other thing about Mr. Javizhi was that although his mastery of the English Language was unquestionable, he was not good at any other language, not even pidgin which everyone else spoke. He could not speak Banakuf, the language of the village. When asked why, he said "I don't even speak Balum which is the language of my own village.

***

On the first day of the second term, Mr. Javizhi noticed that there was a new boy in his class. "Come here!" he said to the little boy. As the latter left his seat and walked towards the teacher, he watched the boy. He was by far the smallest in

44

the class – at least, he looked so. He wore an innocent, almost naïve look on his face. The teacher felt there was something special about this boy, but he could not say what it was.

"Are you a member of this class?"

"Yes, sir."

"How do you know that? You could be in Class 6 A"

"No, sir. I have already been to that class. The teacher looked at his register and said my name was not on it. He said that since he did not have my name, I must be in your class."

"I see. What's your name?"

"Fan, sir."

"What fan? Is your name fan?"

"Yes, sir!"

"Do you know what a fan is?"

"Yes, sir. But my name is spelt with a capital 'F', sir."

"Ah Ha! I see! That's clever. Where have you been? Why have you started the school year half way? Where were you in the first term?"

"I was sick, sir."

"Sick of what? What was wrong with you?"

"I don't know, sir. But the doctors used a needle to get some liquid from my sides."

"Were you coughing?"

"Yes, sir."

"A lot?"

"Yes, sir."

"That sounds like chronic tuberculosis. Are you feeling better now?"

"I think I am well, sir."

"Of course, you are. If you weren't you wouldn't be discharged from hospital. I must say you look very fit."

After checking his register, Mr Javizhi aid to Fan: "That's right. Here is your name, Fan Ndi. Fan is an interesting first name which I haven't heard anywhere else. You may return to your seat."

One day, as the teacher was teaching, Fan suddenly felt like vomiting. His mouth became filled with sputum. Afraid to get up and go to the teacher for permission to go out, he remained seated until the situation started getting out of hand. At last, he plucked courage and stood up. He got to the front of the class but before he could reach the teacher, metabolic matter welled up his stomach like molten lava from a fissure in a rocky mountain. Unable to control it, he opened his mouth and a long jet was thrown up. He vomited about three mouthfuls and then collapsed. Instinctively, most of the pupils in the class stood up in sympathy, some exclaiming. The girls particularly screamed like women do when stung. Mr. Javizhi shouted orders to a girl who was at the front: "Francisca, go and get the First Aid Mistress!"

About three minutes later, Fan had got up by himself, although he had struggled to do so. The teacher did not get upset with him. He simply asked the boy, with commendable composure: "

"What did you eat this morning?"

"Garri, sir."

"Take this and clean your mouth." He said, offering him his own handkerchief.

"Thank you, sir."

Just then, a girl left her seat.

"Where are you going, Florence?"

"To get a bucket and some water to clean the floor, sir."

"Oh, then go ahead, child! It's very thoughtful of you."

That incident drew Mr Javizhi to Fan whom he saw as a frail, vulnerable, innocent and naïve, but nice boy who needed protection which he was ready to provide.

From then on, he would send Fan to work in his house whenever there was manual labour at school. On such occasions, he would warn Fan to be careful not to be seen by the headmaster. "He doesn't think children should be sent to teachers' homes to work."

***

One day when a group of villagers was going past on their bicycles laden with plantains, Mr. Javizhi sent Fan to ask Miss Ngwang if she wanted plantains. The answer was "Yes." So, Fan reported back to him and he bought the plantains for the lady teacher. This was the beginning of a long and lasting relationship. The following year both teachers were to get married to each other.

But Miss Ngwang's hand was not a bed of roses for Mr. Javizhi. She nearly ruined the relationship between Mr. Javizhi and Mr. Lukong: although inadvertently. On the first day Mr. Javizhi walked to school, he travelled in the company of Miss Ngwang and Mr. Lukong. All three lived not far from each other, in the urbanized district. He was impressed with her "exquisite beauty, gentle, in fact, queenly manner and soft-spoken nature," as he put it in a letter to his brother, Francis, who was a civil servant in the north of the country. However, Mr. Javizhi decided to proceed cautiously, not knowing if Miss Ngwang was already committed or not. So in order to find out if Mr. Lukong was involved, as he had observed they had spent some time talking to each other, he asked him one day:

"Are you there, Mr. Lukong? I wonder whether you really ever get the time to do some exercise with the family before leaving for school every morning."

"Exercise in the morning? Forget it! It's my wife who likes such things. She gets the children to do what she calls aerobics, listening to music and following its rhythm while exercising."

"What does your wife do?"

"She teaches at the Government Primary School."

"I see. I don't think about things like that since I live alone and have no one to motivate me."

Miss Ngwang who happened to have joined them, asked: "You mean you're not married, Mr. Javizhi?"

"No, I'm not. I'm still single and available" he said, laughing. Through this brief conversation, Mr. Javizhi had established one fact: Mr. Lukong was married, so eh could now safely go out with Miss Ngwang.

However, what he did not know was that Miss Ngwang and Mr. Lukong did have something going between them. Prior to Mr. Javizhi's arrival, Miss Ngwang who had been at the school for two years and was found to be very pretty, had been the object of courtship of nearly all the male teachers. But secretly she found Mr Lukong the most attractive of all. But since he was married, she held back. Having decided after a year and a half that enough was enough, she finally decided to accompany Mr. Lukong to Mandon the provincial capital, that weekend. He had been asking her for months.

The whole thing came as a joke when during one lunchtime, Mr. Lukong walked towards Miss Ngwang as she sat alone on a chair facing her classroom, knitting a table cover. As he got nearer her (she was backing him), it suddenly occurred to him that it would be more fun if he tiptoed. So he approached her in that manner. The next thing Miss Ngwang knew was that a pair of hands closed in on her and rested firmly on her eyes so that all she could see was darkness. As people usually do when they are blindfolded in that manner, she groped in the dark and felt the hands that were depriving her of sight.

"I think I know whose hands these are. First they are not a woman's hands. They are hairy and too large. And... and if they are ...they are a man's hands, I think I know who it is. Mr. Makombe, please own up because I know it's you! She paused to see if her 'tormentor' would let go. That did not happen. So, she went on: "Then, who is it? Whoever it is let go of me!" Mr. Lukong released her, laughing: "Why did you think it was Mr. Makombe?"

"I don't know. I just called his name. I don't know why. But Mr. Lukong, you scared the life out of me."

"You see, I was just testing your nervous system. Mary, what are you doing on Saturday?"

"Saturday? Nothing special. Whys?"

"I would like you to accompany me to town. I need to purchase a few things there."

"At what time?"

"Well, I reckon that if we leave at 10 o'clock, we should be back by PM. Taxis are very frequent at those times.

"Alright, I'll come." Miss Ngwang's response came as if it was unplanned and spontaneous. But it was not. She had already made up her mind to go out with Mr. Lukong. Nonetheless, she had forgotten that she had rejected all her previous advances. It was on that day that they started going out with each other. And this was before Mr. Javizhi came to the school and set eyes on Miss Mary Ngwang.

Just as Mr. Javizhi fell in love with Miss Ngwang, she too fell in love with him. The first day she saw hi, she could not believe her eyes. She found him to e just the kind of man she had been looking for as a husband. She had always said her ideal mad was one who was tall, of strong build, fair-skinned, handsome, smart, and intelligent and had a sense of humour. Here was that man at last, handed her on a platter of gold. She felt that God in deed, answered prayers. The only problem she had now was that she was still seeing Mr. Lukong. And she did not know how to end the relationship.

It was not long before a certain incident gave the uncomfortable woman the opportunity to state clearly and openly that Mr. Javizhi was the man she preferred. It was a Tuesday afternoon and she was walking back home in the company of Mr. Javizhi and Mr. Lukong and a few other colleagues. In the course of their conversation, Miss Ngwang said: "

"Do you gentlemen know it's my birthday on Saturday?"

"Oh! Is it? And what do you plan to do about it?" asked Javizhi.

"So how old will you be, then?" Mr Lukong asked, almost at the same time as Mr. Javizhi.

"Come on, Mr Lukong! You know you should not ask how old a lady is." snapped Miss Ngwang.

"Alright, I'm sorry!"

"So what are you planning to do to mark your birthday?" asked Mr. Javizhi.

"Nothing special." replied Miss Ngwang.

"In that case, I have a proposal. Let's go on a picnic. Just you and me." answered Mr Javizhi.

"No, I have a better idea. Let's take a trip to town." Mr. Lukong said, as if to contradict Mr. Javizhi.

"Oh no! Not you, Mr. Lukong. You're a married man. I'll accept Mr. Javizhi's offer. I'm a lot safer with him."

Mr. Lukong got the message and from that day, reduced his love interest in Miss Ngwang more and more. Mr. Javizhi took the upper hand to strengthen his own relationship with Miss Ngwang at the least opportunity. Within six months, they were married. The wedding took place in his village in the presence of his family. However, none of his colleagues was able to travel to see the ceremony. But when the couple returned to school, the staff made a contribution of some money and gave them a reception. From that day and like a real gentleman, Mr. Lukong reviewed his affiliation to Mr. and Mrs. Javizhi. The former became his best friend, and the latter, a valuable colleague.

***

Mr. Javizhi continued to keep and eye on Fan, the new boy who joined his class at the beginning of the second term. This was in fact, his pet pupil, not because he was very bright – he wasn't, but because he had something about him that made the teacher just like him. He was quiet, shy, looked "sharp" as Mr. Javizhi would say, and inspired trust. As a result, Mr Javizhi kept sending him to work in his house whenever there was manual labour at school. Each time Mrs. Javizhi needed something from her husband across the road in her own classroom; it was always Fan that her husband sent to her.

Nonetheless, one day, Mr. Javizhi lost his patience with Fan. The class was doing geometry when as the teacher walked about looking at what pupils were doing; he stopped at Fan's desk. Touching the boy's book with his stick, he said: "This angle is too small. Cross out the square and start all over. Remember that all the angles in a square are equal." The teacher then walked away.

Some ten minutes later, he returned only to find that the boy had neither crossed out the wrong diagram nor started a new one.

"What are you doing? I told you to cross out this square and start another one! What's wrong with you? This child; you have no sense of proportion. I want you to do as you are told; otherwise, I'll keep you back after school."

When Mr. Javizhi compiled his class results for the term, he realized that although Fan was always sick throughout the previous term, he still passed the examination. Even so, it was a poor pass. The young man was 30th out of 45. The teacher commented in his report card: "Fan needs encouragement. He has passed his exams, which is commendable, considering that he was away in the first term."

Later in the year, when the third term results - the most important as they decided whether a child would be promoted or not — Fan's results were, unfortunately not very different from the second term's. He was 29th out of 45. The remark in his report card was: "Fan has worked hard this term. However, because of the work he missed in the first term, he has not been able to achieve his maximum. Consequently, although he passed to Class 7, I am of the opinion that he repeats Class Six in order to regain the lost ground."

Report cards were given out after results had been announced at the school assembly. Classes 5, 6 and 7 , called Upper School, usually had their own assembly while Classes 1, 2, 3 and 4 which constituted Junior School, had theirs separately. When Mr. Javizhi read out Fan's name as one of the successful ones, he did not say that the boy was being asked to repeat Class 6. So like all the other children who knew they had been promoted, Fan rejoiced. Yet, shortly after school had been dismissed, Mr Javizhi called him aside and broke the news to him. Feeling he had sufficiently prepared the boy's mind, he handed him his report card and left. Hoping that what the teacher told him wasn't true, Fan opened his report card, but there it was in black and white. It was therefore a very upset Fan who went home that afternoon.

As soon as Fan got home, his father asked:

"Fan, did you pass your exams?"

"Yes, Papa. "

"But you don't look happy my son. What's the matter?" inquired his mother.

"The teacher says I should repeat Class 6."

"Why should he say that if you passed?" his father asked.

"Because he says it wasn't a good pass."

"Well, don't worry about it. I'm going to see him tomorrow and ask him to explain."

When Fan's father spoke to the teacher, he found his reasons for the decision very reasonable. So, he said to the teacher: "I agree with you. It's in his interest to repeat Class 6."

***

On the first day of the new school year, as Fan was entering the Senior Section, Mr. Javizhi spotted him and sent a boy to call him. When he got to the teacher, he found that he was standing near the assembly ground with an unknown man who must be a new teacher. Turning to the latter, Mr. Javizhi said: "Mr. Nfor, this is the boy I told you about."

Mr. Nfor then said to Fan: "You passed your promotion exam, which is a good thing. However, I agree with Mr. Javizhi that you should repeat Class 6. You are still small and considering that you are also intelligent, I am sure that if you repeat, you will top the class."

The point about topping the class caught Fan's attention more than any other reason for repeating he and been given. He imagined how he would feel if at the end of the year when results were being announced, he came first in his class. Surely, that would be wonderful!

Fan's teacher in Class 6 in that year was a new one called Mr. Cosmas Amougou. Mr. Javizhi had been moved up to Class 7. %or. Nfor was one of the Class 5 teachers.

From Fan's point of view, the year ended very quickly. Perhaps it was because he had a very busy time. Firstly, he was determined to top his class. His anxiety was increased when it was announced that Classes 6A and Six B would both write the same exam and be graded and classified like one class. This meant he would not be competing with just a score and a half other pupils but twice that number.

His determination paid off as when the Class Six First Term results were announced, what he had been hoping for was what he heard. When his new teacher, Mr. Cosmas, as pupils called him, stepped forward to announce the Class 6 results, he said:

"Firstly, I would like to ell you that these results are those of Class 6 'A' and Class 6 'B', combined. The first in the class is…Fan Ndi! He …"

"That my child, eh! That my child eh! "Cried out Mr Javizhi with excitement as he stepped forward. "Some of you will remember that this boy was in this class last year. He was actually promoted to Class 7 but I advised him to repeat because he was away throughout the first term. I am glad that he has done so well!"

Encouraged by his performance, Fan decided to write the Common Entrance Examination into secondary schools the following term. When he mentioned it to his parents they agreed he should if he really wanted to. Even Mr. Javizhi, who had by now firmly established himself as Fan's guardian at school, supported the idea.

The Common Entrance Exam was written towards the end of the second term, marked during the Easter break and the results released at the beginning of the third term. Interviews into specific colleges were conducted later. Fan took a lot of people by surprise by passing both the written exam and the interview. Mr. Javizhi was so pleased that he ran around asking every teacher he could find: "Have you heard the news? Have you heard the news? That my child has done it again!" To crown it all, Fan was again the first in the class in the second and third terms. Mr. Javizhi's joy was total.

One afternoon after school, Mr Javizhi called Fan back as he was about to leave for home: "Fan, how do you feel about passing the Common Entrance?"

"I am happy, Sir. I am very happy."

"And how does your father feel about it?"

"He is very happy, too, Sir."

"So, are you going to college in September, or you are coming back to St. John's to do Class 7?"

"I think I will go, Sir. "

"I think you should, Fan. I would like you to come to my house on Saturday afternoon so that my wife and I can tell you about secondary school life. You will find that it's very different from what you knew before."

"I will come on Saturday, Sir. At what time should I come, Sir?"

"Any time after 2 O'clock. We're not going anywhere. We'll be indoors."

***

Fan got his Common Entrance interview result a month and a half before the end of the school year. Two weeks later, Mr. Javizhi also received good news when he was informed that he was the only teacher in the whole province that had passed the exam into the country's prestigious education institute to read education management. He would be at the institution for one year during which he would be on full salary. At the end of the course he would be appointed to a management position where he could earn three times his teacher's salary.

News of Fan's impending departure for secondary school met with awe from his classmates who were only now really beginning to wake up to the fact that he would no longer be with them from September. However, Fan himself felt he had simply got back what was his by right. This was because as he put it, the Class 7 pupils who were also passing out at the end of year were his rightful classmates and not those of Class 6 where he was.

As might be expected, the main star of the show was Mr. Javizhi. News of his own success caused a stir, not only at the school but throughout the village and beyond. Teacher after teacher congratulated him. Some regretted that volleyball would be a thing of the past. Pupils kept asking him if he could not turn down the offer and stay on at St. John's. He asked them:

"Why do you want me to stay?"

A girl said: "Because we like you, Sir."

"Why do you like me?"

"Because you are a good teacher, Sir."

"What makes you say I'm a good teacher, Janet?"

"You teach well, Sir. You don't insult us, you are caring and you make us laugh."

"Really?" Mr. Javizhi responded, smiling as if to say, "Tell me more."

"It's true, Sir." She said.

"Thank you for that. I only wish I could stay. But this offer I have is an opportunity of a lifetime."

The headmaster summed up the mood when he said in his farewell speech: "Those who have been long at this school like Miss Ngome, Mr. Yufanyi and Mrs Njikam agree with me that never before has St. John's had a teacher of such a calibre like Mr. Javizhi. He is dynamic, efficient and very popular with pupils, colleagues and parents. I recall that only a few days ago, a parent came to my office and said he had heard the good news about Mr. Javizhi. He said his daughters in Classes 7 and 6 spoke so positively about Mr. Javizhi that he was thinking of giving him his older daughter for a wife. I told him that it was a very good gesture which I was sure Mr. Javizhi would appreciate. However, I pointed out to the parent that Mr. Javizhi was already married, he told me he was aware of that but was sure his daughter would make an excellent second wife." H e was interrupted by the laughter of his colleagues. "Ladies and gentlemen," he went on, "Ladies and gentlemen, I have been headmaster in this school for seven years but no parent has ever offered me a second wife. So you will understand me if I say I'm beginning to be jealous of Mr. Javizhi. Anyway, I'm sure I speak for all of us when I say we wish Mr. Javizhi the very best in his new station. Thank you very much."

As soon as a round of applause had been given to the headmaster, Mr. Javizhi was urged to take the floor. One could hear colleagues imploring him to speak: "Speech! Speech!" "Give a response to the HM's speech!" "Come on! Come on!" Mr. Javizhi stepped forward. "Mary, please! Where is Mrs. Javizhi?" His wife also stepped ahead and stood next to him. Mr. Javizhi placed his hand on his wife's shoulder and said: "Thank you very much for the speech,

HM. I must say I'm so moved that I lack words to express myself. However, I must say that I have profoundly enjoyed the two years I have spent here. I would like to believe that I have made lasting friends in this school and this village. Do not forget this was where I met my lovely and beautiful wife. I came here as a bachelor but I'm now returning a married man. That shows that I have matured while here. I will never forget St. John's or Banakuf."

This happened on the last day of the third term, and therefore of the school year, after pupils had been given their results. Thereafter, teachers dispersed to wait for two and a half months before coming to start another school year. For Mr. John Javizhi and his little boy, Fan, this was also their very last day at the school.

5

The Money

Mami Aggie had a problem on her hands and knew this only too well. A mother of seven, she used to say that she had more than her fair share of troubles, compared with other mothers with the same number of children. Yet, the strange thing is that her troubles – nearly all of the – came from one and the same child. The author of Mami Aggie's misfortunes was Bala, a boy, and the third of her children. The other children were, in order of birth, Aggie, Peter, Ann, Helen, Sarah and Anthony.

Bala stole a lot. In fact, he stole foolishly and some times he would take articles for which he had little or no use. He was well known for this in the compound – a fairly large one as his father, Pa Ezekiel, had three other wives, one of whom had three children and the other two had four and three respectively. Pa Ezekiel whom, some believed had fathered all nineteen children yet others believe some were the products of secret lovers of his wives, was a strict man who did not believe in sparing the rod and spoiling the child. He tried all kinds of methods to get Bala to change his ways but failed. Not even repeated corporal punishment worked. And so the boy continued to steal, from slices of meat in pots of soup or cubes of sugar at home, to pencils, pens, erasers, rulers and books at school.

Usually when Bala was caught in the act and his father was giving him a beating; his mother would throw up her hands and cry out as if speaking directly to God:

"Why me, Lord? Why me? What have I done to deserve this?"

His father would say as the whip fell on him:

"Yes, yes, I told you but you wouldn't listen! Stealing is bad! It isn't good at all. You must abandon it. You have brought disgrace on this family. You have made everyone view you as nothing else but a thief. And that is very bad for you."

***

After returning from church that Sunday early afternoon, Mami Aggie gave the children food and hurried off to her 'njangi' which was in another compound in the village. She could not afford to be late because being the treasurer, she played a key role. The 'njangi' worked in two ways. Firstly when members met, which was monthly, they each contributed FCFA 5000. and once money from all ten members who were all women was collected, the president was then charged by the rest of the group to receive the money after it had been counted by the treasurer and the beneficiary, and then formally present it to the latter, amidst a round of applause. The second part of the 'njangi' consisted of each member handed an unspecified amount of money to the treasurer for savings. The amount here was sometimes fairly large as members could also open accounts for relatives, including children, who were not present. After all members had handed their savings to the treasurer, she then took them home. The following day, Monday, she took the money to the bank in the nearby town, Nkolbon. On this Sunday, she collected a total of FCFA 68 200. She put it in her handbag and when the meeting broke up, she went straight home. As soon as entered her house, an old friend of hers whom she had not seen for a long time paid her a surprise visit.

"Aggie!"

"Who am I seeing here? Am I dreaming?"

"Oh no! You're not! It's me your old friend!"

"But Jane, where have you been? We haven't seen each other for years!"

"Yes, twelve years, to be exact."

"I know you left the village and got married to this man from the economic capital. But I never saw you again."

By this time, the two women had run into each other's arms and were admiring each other as they spoke.

"But Aggie, you haven't changed one bit. And my God, how you look good!"

"Oh well, I try. But you know I have seven children. How many do you have?

"Oh my dear friend, I have five. "

"Five! You aren't doing badly at all. What do you do in Madungu, Jane?"

"I do petty trading. I run a provision store and a small restaurant attached to it."

By now, the two women were sitting in Mami Aggie's bedroom. Her husband was an enlightened polygamist who provided each of his wives with a bedroom, a sitting room and a kitchen.

"I also do trading. I buy foodstuff from all over the village and sell in Nkolbon town." Aggie told her friend. They spent the rest of the afternoon together, chatting and chatting. At about eight o'clock, Jane said she was leaving.

"No, no Jane. You haven't eaten yet. Oh dear, we spent so much time talking that I forgot to give you something to eat."

"Don't worry, Aggie. This house is as much mine as it is yours. If I had wanted food I would have helped myself."

"It's alright for you to say that. Even so, the fact remains that you haven't eaten. Never mind. I will prepare something quick for you. Ann! I mean, Helen! No, Grace!"

"Yes, mama!" Grace came running.

"Please, put some water on the fire and bring some 'foo foo' corn powder quickly."

After the meal, Mami Aggie left with her friend.

"I am going to see off Auntie Jane, just in case Papa wants me." She told the children. As the two women walked away they continued conversing and exchanging gossips. Mami Aggie had been away for another half hour when she suddenly stopped short as if something had gone wrong.

"What is it, Aggie?"

"It's the money. Jane, it's our 'njangi' money. I left it in my bag in the sitting room and I'm not sure it's safe."

"In that case, I think you should return home fast."

***

Mami was out of breath when she got home. She dived straight into the sitting room and grabbed her handbag; it was still where she had left it. But when she opened it, the money was gone.

"I knew it! I knew it! "She kept saying as she emptied the bag and searched every nook and cranny of it. She was just being desperate,; otherwise she knew perfectly well that since the money had been put in a white envelope before being placed in the bag, she should have found the envelope almost as soon as she opened the bag.

The poor woman let out a loud yell: "What misfortune is this? Why didn't I take the money with me?"

Turning to the children, she asked: "Where is Papa?"

He hasn't returned since he went out in the afternoon, mama."

"Okay. This means I have to deal with the matter myself. Where is Bala? Bala! Bala!"

"He was here a while ago. I don't know where he has gone."

"Yes, of course; how can he be here after doing what he has done? Find him at once!" About five minutes later, Bala came in, on his own. At once his mother grabbed him:

"Where is the money? Bring me that money!"

"What money, mama? I don't know anything about any money."

"Of course, you do. You removed that money from my bag. It was njangi money I just collected today. You took it; so don't start lying to me.

"I didn't take it, mama. I didn't even see it. I didn't know you had money."

"You are lying. How have you known in the past where things are before stealing them? Alright, come outside with me and I'll teach you how to say the truth!" she threatened, as she dragged the boy out in the yard. "Helen, bring me a whip!"

When Mami got the cane, she landed it on Bala's back. As she whipped him, she spoke: "I don't know what kind of a child…you are. I have …had enough…enough trouble from you…Bala. It's too much to come from one child. But the worse is…The worst is that …you could do to me is steal 'njangi' money. This is… This is … other people's money…Not mine. Not mine. So you have put… put me in deep trouble."

Bala was screaming at the top of his voice. The other women in the compound came out to se what was going on and realising that it was Bala, they immediately re-entered their houses, the interpretation being that if it was Bala, he must have stolen something yet again. Having struck the boy for so long and so hard that her hand hurt, Mami Aggie decided to rest a little. Meanwhile in order to tighten the screw on Bala while she rested, she placed a piece of wood behind his knees and ordered him to sit with his buttocks near the floor but not touching it. This made the knees and legs hurt a lot. Bala was still weeping and proclaiming his innocence. To his mother, it was crocodile tears.

After about some twenty minutes, Mami Aggie returned to the accused: "Are you now prepared to tell the truth or should I cane you some more?"

"I have already told you the truth, mama. I don't know anything about the money."

"Fine; Then I'll continue beating you." She said. At once she started lashing out at him again: "I knew… I knew you would say that…But I know you took the money. Only you…Only you could have taken it…as … as you have taken so many other things before…"

"No, no, mama. It wasn't me. I swear it wasn't me. «Stop lying…stop it. And don't swear. God does not like children who steal, let alone those who steal and then tell lies."

At that point, Bala collapsed and passed out. His mother panicked. She ran around like a mad woman, not knowing what to do. Then picking up her child and holding him to her chest, she sobbed saying: "Oh my God! What have I done? What is money that I should kill my own child? What has come over me?"

By now, the other wives in the compound and some neighbours who had heard Mami Aggie's cry for help were at the scene. Two male neighbours were trying to re-animate Bala by dousing him with cold water. Finally, he came to. Noticing this, his mother ran towards her son, put her hound round his neck and said: "Dear child, forgive me. All of that money can't replace you. I'll work hard and pay it back."

Just then, a neighbour dragged her little boy – about Bala's age, through the crowd to the middle where Mami Aggie was clutching hr son and shedding tears.

"Confess!" Mami Peter, for that was her name, yelled as she pushed her son forward. "Tell Bala's mother it was you who stole the money. Tell her. Or do you want another beating?" Mama Peter said as she raised her hand as if to strike him again.

"No, mother. I will tell her."

Without waiting for the boy to speak, Bala's mother asked Peter: "Was it you who took the money?"

"Yes, mama. I am sorry." Peter replied, remorsefully.

"I am sorry, Aggie. Here is your money. I counted it. It is exactly FCFA 68 200. Is that how much it was?" asked Peter's mother.

"Yes, it is. It is. I can't believe I've found this money. My God is a good God, in deed. Oh thank you so much!" Mami Aggie said as she embraced Mami Peter and Peter too. Turning to her son who was now on his feet but still in too much pain to fully grasp what was going on, Mami Aggie looked him straight in the face and told him: "Forgive me my son. I'm sorry I treated you in this way. Come and I'll give you a warm bath to soothe your aching body."

6

Moment of Truth

Fondem belonged to a group of friends who grew up in the village together. They were 'kang', pronounced so that the intonation falls like in the English word, 'for', when uttered in isolation. Translated into English, therefore: 'kang' means, "Age mate." Ordinarily this applies to people who are of the same age. However, in practice, some can be up to three or even four years older. Usually when this happens it can be because existing members deliberately want to increase their numbers in order to look strong in the face of other 'kang' groups. Another reason is that sometimes postulants who normally would not be admitted in a 'kang' because they are under-aged or over-aged, find a way of 'buying' membership and thus 'close' the mouths of those existing members who would have protested. Often, members justified this beefing up of membership by claiming that 'there's safety in numbers'. There were in all, nine members in Fondem's 'kang', with the other members being Alos, Akum, Muma, Achiri, Ngu, Nji, Cho and Mokom.

This day in question being the weekly market day, Mbon, all nine mates as usual, found themselves in their njangi hut. On Mbon practically everyone went to the market, as this was a good opportunity to socialize. As the nine deliberated, chatted, drank palm wine from cups made out of cow horns that had been skilfully polished, the rest of the market rumbled on regardless. Men, women and children went about their business. Some haggled and bought, others moved on to the next vendor. Those who sold stuck to their guns and finally settled for a price that was convenient to them. Buyers too clinched deals here and there as they tried to outwit vendors.

Back in the 'Akongni' (Love) hut, as the meeting house of the nine was called, the men had just finished the financial aspect of their business.

The happy man for the week was none other than Fondem. He was the week's beneficiary of the FCFA 2500 saved by each member and jointly given to one member according to a roster that had been drawn up for the purpose. Excluding the recipient's contribution which was usually waived, each receiver collected a total of FCFA 20 000. This was a unique interest-free loan made available to each member when his turn came. Nonetheless, Akongni was not the only such group in the village.

After Fondem put the money away after counting it carefully to ascertain that the amount was correct, Mokom spoke:

"*Iye*, Fondem. Why do you just put the money away without asking us your elders to advise you on how to spend it?"

Fondem replied: "Here! Here! Mokom is older than me by only eight months, yet he thinks he is my elder!"

Muma joined in: "Of course, he is your elder. I am only a week older than Mokom. Yet there is no doubt that I am his elder. If he and I ate achoo from the same leaf, I would choose my slice of meat before he chose his and this by virtue of the slight difference in our ages. Again if Mokom and I slept on the same bed, I would be the one to sleep at the front, and he at the back. And this is because I am older, albeit by only one week. So you see, Fondem, you ought to ask us, your elders, advice about spending your money. Even if …"

At this juncture, Alos who was the oldest of the 'kang' spoke:

"Enough! Enough, all of you! Why must you make so much noise about age when you know I am present? When I saw the light of day none of you had been born. So who better is here to advise Fondem?"

"No! No! Alos!" protested Nji.

"Who are you addressing as 'Alos'? Can't you show your elders some respect?"

"Elders? Who are my elders here? We are age-mates; aren't we?" Nji asked, looking round for support.

"Yes, we are age-mates!" Chorused at least five of them.

"Listen to me, all of you." Cut in Fondem. "It is about me you are quarrelling. So I think it is only fair that I should say what I think." Another round of chorus urged him on: "Speak, we are listening!"

"Alright, what I think is that we should listen to Alos and find out exactly what he wants to tell us. I think it is his birth right as the oldest in our group. However, if he talks nonsense, we won't hesitate to shoot it down, shall we?" said Fondem.

There was loud laughter from nearly everybody.

Before it subsided, Alos had again risen to his feet in order not to miss his chance. "Alright, mates! Alright! Imagine Fondem readily allowing me to speak when in previous meetings he has been the first to stop me on the grounds that although I may be the oldest of us, I am the shortest. So, what has come over him today, all of a sudden? Ah! I think I know. Have I not always said if you give man money, you can get him to do whatever you want, even if it means raping his own mother? Ha!" Angered by that remark, Fondem also rose but was shouted down by some mates.

"Sit down! Sit down! Let Alos speak. You have had your chance. If you wish to take the floor again, you must wait for him to finish. In any case it was you who asked him to speak. So you brought it upon yourself."

Fondem sat down, but not before pointing a warning finger at Alos and muttering something. Alos went on.

"Regarding the money Fondem has collected today, I would have advised him to get another wife since he is the only member of this 'kang' with only two wives. However, knowing him, he won't do such a thing. I know he will buy more presents for Anyoh, his second wife whom he likes so much. Do you ..." Ngu, the second oldest, two days younger than Alos, spoke.

"Alos, listen. Why don't we first of all let Fondem tell us what he intends to do with the money? Come on, Fondem. Tell us! Come on and tell us! You know that in this group we are like brothers. We don't hide anything from each other, or do we, mates?"

"No, we don't!" came the response.

"Fine! Fine! If you must know, then I'll tell you. With this money, I'll build a new house for Anyoh's mother. I'll ..."

The group broke loose as if the devil had suddenly possessed them. Some got up and screamed, others stamped their feet in anger, others burst out laughing. Akum, the most outspoken said:

"I knew it! I knew it had to be something like that. It must be either Anyoh or her mother or her father. It's as if Fondem's first wife; Anjei, did not exist. I'm sure this Anyoh had bewitched our dear brother here. Otherwise, how can anyone explain why it's always Anyoh? A few months ago he bought her a sewing machine while Anjei had none, although she is the senior wife. He has started a petty trading business for Anyoh while Anjei is let to till the farms. Yet, yet, this Anyoh doesn't have a child, not one, whereas Anjei has given him five, with two boys, which means Fondem is sure to have a successor if he dies today. This little queen of his is sterile. She is barren."

"Akum shut up and sit down! You don't know what you're talking about. Sit down!" Fondem shouted as he launched a physical assault at Akum. Alos and Muma stepped in early and stopped the fight. Alos, in his capacity as the eldest and de facto chairman of the group asked everyone to take their seats and reminded members of the group's rules regarding gentlemanly behaviour. He then ordered Fondem to publicly apologise to Akum and pay a fine of a jug of palm wine for attempted assault. The former complied.

When the wine had been served, Alos invited Fondem to resume his explanation of what he would do with the money. He warned him about proper behaviour.

"Thank you for giving me the floor, Mr Chairman. As I said earlier, I intend to build a house for Anyoh's mother with this money." Akum asked to speak, to which Alos said: "No, not you again, Akum. Let somewhere else speak. Someone who hasn't spoken much this evening. Yes, Cho. You can speak."

"Thank you. I have one question for Fondem. What has Anyoh got that Anjei hasn't?" Cho asked Fondem.

"Yes, I can tell you. Anyoh loves me with all her heart. Anjei is with me only for my money and belongings."

Cho spoke again: "That's an outrage! The one on whom you spend so much money is the real exploiter. Can't you see? Or has she blinded you?"

Muma stepped forward excitedly. Listen to me, everyone. I have a solution to all this." His enthusiasm was so much that Alos did not stop him from speaking. Muma went on: "But first, one question for Fondem. *Iye*, are you sure Anyoh is the one who loves you with all her heart?"

"Of course, I'm sure about it. I've been married to Anjei for eighteen years and to Anyoh for six years. So I know both women thoroughly."

"That's alright! That's alright! If you agree, I'll recommend to you a little straightforward test that will lead us to the truth. Do you agree?" Before Fondem could say anything, the group chorused: "Accept it! Accept it! Say yes!"

"Okay. I accept."

"Akum outlined the plan to Fondem and the other members of the group. It was exciting and left each of them eager to know what the outcome would be.

***

It was the day of the week known in Ngamambo, the language of the village, as 'Ku'. When pronounced the name sounds like the name given to the little lumps one finds in achoo that has not been pounded well.

Following Fondem's instructions, Anjei had taken all her children with her to the two-mile away farm at Njini Menam. That is, all her children except the first two who were away in college. Anjei was told that she had to be home at about 6 p.m. for a family meeting. Anyoh had been sent to Mbenchom, her mother's village some five miles away, to inform her that Fondem would be bringing workmen to commence work on the house the following week. Like Anjei, Anyoh was told she had to be home by 6 p.m. for a family meeting. None of the women could imagine why there had to be a family meeting on this day. Their husband rarely held such meetings unless there was something urgent to be announced or discussed. Before Anyoh came into the family, Fondem had held a meeting only once with Anjei and the three children who had been born at the time. Anjei was informed she would be having a "partner" to help her in her duties as housewife. The children were told they would have "another mother." Curious, the oldest child, a girl named Anwei, then aged 11, asked her father: "Papa, does that mean we won't be having mama anymore?"

"No, child. It means you will have two mothers, your present mother and the new one whom you must also call, 'mother'."

***

Anyoh was the first of the two wives to return home that evening. As she approached the compound, for some reason, she had a strange feeling. Her hair stood and she felt her heart pounding. As she entered the compound, it appeared to her that there was a human figure lying in the yard as if it had been assaulted. But it was motionless. As she got nearer, she discovered it was her husband. He was lying on the ground face up, his intestines lying on his belly and blood splashed all over his body and on the ground. She stood for a few seconds and stared at her dead husband. But she was emotionless. Then as if stung, she rushed into her husband's own house and started moving out the most prized of his belongings. She did not alert anybody about the death.

Then came Anjei with her children. The first thing she noticed was Anyoh struggling with her husband's things. From a distance, Anjei watched her remove goods from her husband's house and stack them in the yard, ostensibly with the intention of carrying them away. Anjei wondered what was going on.

As she went nearer, she noticed her husband on the earthen floor. At once she let out a shriek, exclaiming: "Help! Help! My husband is dead!" She ran around screaming and weeping, her children with her. As she wondered loudly what she would do without her beloved children, the children cried: "Father, why have you done this? Come back! Come back! We need you!" While all this was happening, Anyoh who had not shed a single tear was busy carrying away from the compound the things she had stacked up. She even

73

brought a man and a woman; perhaps friends, perhaps relatives, to help her move the things out quickly, as if she feared that by some miracle her husband might come back to life and stop her.

Just as Anyoh and her two friends had loaded the things on their heads and were about to leave the gates of the compound, Fondem suddenly got up and the intestines dropped on the ground.

'Anjei, don't cry! I'm not dead. I'm alive. Now I know you are the woman who loves me. Anyoh never loved me, yet I wouldn't accept this. Well, Anyoh, since you have shown me your true colours, I ask you to take with you the things you have collected. But you must never set foot on this compound any more. It's over between you and me."

On hearing these words, Anyoh began to cry and say that she loved her husband. Even so, she could not pull the wool over Fondem's eyes any more.

"Who do you want to deceive again? There's no need to shed crocodile's tears. When you saw me lying here looking dead, why didn't you cry like Anjei? I won't be a fool twice." Turning to the over one hundred villagers, who hearing Anjei's cries for help, had come rushing, Fondem said:

"Good people, thank you very much for coming. As you can see, this was a faked death. I had a bet with my 'kang'. While they knew that Anjei loved me truly, I was foolish enough to think that it was my second wife who loved me. In order for me to find out which of my wives really loved me, we decided I'd lie in the yard with chicken intestines on my stomach and blood all over me to see which of the wives would show more concern. The result has been clear to all of us. Please, sit down and let's drink to celebrate for you are true friends of mine. If I had died in reality, I have no doubt that you'd have been here as you are now to bury and mourn me in the proper way. I must thank my 'kang', especially Muma who devised this waterproof formula which as you can see, worked. Anjei, my wife, my one and only wife, please, come forward. I don't know how to thank you. However, in gratitude to your mother for giving birth to someone like you, I'll build her a house with the money I collected from my mates on Mbon."

7

Caught In-between

Christ the Saviour College (CSC) was a much sought-after institution which attracted large numbers of students from both far and near. The twenty year old educational institution had made its mark in academia, having produced some of the best GCE 'O' and 'A' Level results in the country. However, perhaps its strongest point was its Christian ethos which permeated all aspects of life on the college premises. A boarding school for boys, it was conceived, designed, built and run by Catholic missionaries from England.

Perched on a hill which made this famous institution visible from any angle of Luluan town, it stood out as a constant reminder of the creator to whoever viewed it. At night time, its bright lights seen even from afar, reminded the inhabitants of this predominantly catholic town that like the incandescent glow, the light of God in man would shine on, unless man put it out. This point was reinforced by the weekly masses which CSC held for inhabitants of the school environs.

On Sunday mornings, the chaplain and reverend brothers could be seen looking very smart and busy in their immaculately white cassocks.

"Good morning! How you dey? You dong come for church?" Father Smith who was the school's chaplain, principal and head of English, could be heard saying to visiting Christians.

"Morning, Father. I dey fine, sah. I dong come for mass."

Father Smith was the most jovial, ye the most authoritative of all the missionaries at the school – six were European and the two most 'junior' were Cameroonians.

"Hey, you! Come here, boy! Why are you loitering out here when you should be in class? Off you go!" he would say to a student catch idling away. When he was not in such good moods, Father Smith would hit the student before dismissing him in order to 'give you something to remember." As he would put it. Nonetheless, his most lively moment was when he was teaching English. At such times he would leap about, mimic, tiptoe, sing, dance, and whistle or mumble as the need arose.

***

One Tuesday morning as he entered the fifth form for the weekly combined English language lesson, the students immediately knew he had some interesting announcement to make. This was because he looked very happy.

But unfortunately for them they could not tell what it was he wanted to tell them.

"Sit down, boys! Sit down!" he said, waving at them as they all rose to acknowledge his entry in the classroom. "Sit down, please! Now, listen carefully." He said, placing on the table the pile of books he was carrying.

"I have an interesting announcement for you." At once, the 60 boys in the class all went quiet in anticipation.

"I'm pleased to inform you that on the occasion of the feast of the patron saint of our school next month, we are hereby launching an essay competition for you Fifth Form students. The best essay will earn its writer part payment of his tuition fees. The second and third best will each attract lesser cash awards, but cash awards nevertheless. All three will be published in the school magazine. Any questions?" At least ten hands shot up immediately.

"Aha! I can see you like the idea. Now let me answer some questions. Yes, Shey, what's your question?"

"Please, Father, what can we write about?"

"Right, Shey. It's entirely up to you what topic you choose. Only make your essay interesting. Any other questions? You, Ngoran!"

"Please Father; I would like to know when the essays are to be handed in."

"Oh well, let's have them as soon as possible. No, better still, hand them in during this same lesson next week. Is that clear?"

"Yes Father!" they responded with excitement.

"Now, let's get on with today's lesson. Where did we stop last time? Anyone? Yes, Fai."

"Please Father, you were telling us the difference between transitive and intransitive verbs."

"That's right! That's right!"

On the appointed day, Father Smith collected the essays. Practically, every Fifth Former submitted an entry. After the priest had collected all the essays, he said to the students:

"We shall see who will be the winners. We shall see that!"

***

Three days later, while the Fifth Years were having history, Father Smith was seen marching in fury towards the Form 5 'A' classroom. He held a pile of students' scripts in his left hand. His right hand was clenched and as he walked on he waved it angrily and muttered something. The force with which he lifted his feet and put them down (almost stamping them) made the concrete floor thunder. The echo was all the louder as the classroom was situated on the upper of the two floor, the American style. Mr Smith burst into the classroom and ignoring Mr Ngome, the History teacher, he roared:

"Where is that little worm called Andrew? Where is he?"

Mr Ngome, trying to be helpful, looked in Andrew's direction and ordered: "Wayighi, stand up!" The rest of the students held their breath. It was very rarely that Father Smith was ever in this state. So, why, they wondered, was it happening today? What might have happened? What could Andrew Wayighi have done wrong?

"Come here, you little rascal!" Father Smith thundered, pulling Wayighi by the hand.

"Did you write this? Did you?" he asked, waving the boy's essay at him.

"So you did then, eh? Well, come with me!"

As priest and student walked away from the Form Five corridor, it began to be clear to the rest of the students that there must be something wrong with Wayighi's essay. But what it was, they wondered. As soon as Father Smith entered his office, he went round his desk and sat in his chair. Then again, he waved Wayighi's essay, threw it at him and barked: "Read it! Read it to me and make sure you are audible!"

Wayighi picked up the script with trembling hands. He looked at it and opened his mouth but no word came out. So great was his fright!

Just then Reverend Brother Paul opened the door and came in. "Is everything alright, Father?" he inquired.

"Alright, Brother? Oh no! Not with the likes of this ignorant ignoramus here. This is an outrage! How can a child we have brought up in the Christian way write such a dirty essay?"

"Can I see the essay, Father?"

"Of course, Brother Paul." He responded, snatching it from Wayighi. "Here it is, Brother."

When Bro. Paul took the essay from Fr; Smith and looked at it, he whispered something in the ear of the latter. Then turning to Wayighi, Fr. Smith said: "Andrew, you can return to class. I'll send for you later."

After carefully going through the essay, Bro. Paul said to Fr; Smith: "Father, this essay is unacceptable because it's an indictment of the holy work we're doing here. In a way, it is an affront at Christ himself. But at the same time, it is a well written essay."

"Oh yes! There is no doubt that it's well written. In fact, it's the best of all the essays."

"In that case, Father, I suggest that the Disciplinary Committee meets."

"Fine. Then we'll meet tomorrow after school. I'll send a memo round at once."

***

As chairman of the Disciplinary Committee, Fr. Smith spoke first. This was after the opening prayer:

"Gentlemen, before we send for the student in question, let's understand the reason for this impromptu meeting. I have been correcting essays submitted by Fifth Year students in the essay contest I launched to mark the Feast Day of our school. However, one essay has disturbed me profoundly. It's that of Andrew Wayighi whom we will be calling in soon."

"What's the essay about, Father?" inquired one of the members of the committee.

"I will come to that soon, if you will just listen. Basically this little worm has written about a priest who was giving a sermon once during mass and pulled out of his pocket a lady's underwear which he waved to the congregation thinking it was his white handkerchief. Apparently he was saying to the congregation:

"Let your hearts be as pure as this handkerchief. It was the look of consternation on the face of the congregation that alerted him to the odd thing that he was waving and the fact that alarmed. They started leaving the church one by one. It turned out the priest had spent the night in the home of one of his parishioners whose husband was away."

After listening to Fr. Smith, Bro. Paul suggested that the boy should be called in. When he came in, Bro. was the first to address him:

"Andrew?"

"Yes, Brother."

"Did you write this essay?"

"Yes, Brother."

"Did you like it?"

"I don't know, Brother."

"Why did you choose the topic? Do you know it's against the Catholic spirit and philosophy?"

"Father asked us to choose any topic, Brother."

"Yes, but I didn't ask you to write about eroticism. This is absurd!" protested the priest.

"But you asked us to make our essays interesting, Father."

"Shut up and don't argue with me."

Mr Tamfuh, the longest serving teacher at CSC suggested that the deliberations continued without Wayighi. Fr. Smith asked the boy to leave the room. Attention was now turned to how to conclude the case. After deliberating further for an hour, the following steps were taken:

-Wayighi would be warned never to discuss the contents of his essay with anybody.

- His controversial essay would be discreetly withdrawn by the principal

-Because he was such a good English Language student and had hardly got in trouble previously, he would be allowed to submit another essay on a different and more acceptable topic to be approved by Fr Smith.

-Arrangements would be made for him to see Fr. Smith and go to confession after which the man of God would prescribe him penance commensurate with his 'sin'.

8

A Matter of Choice

There was absolutely no doubt that this was a big day in the life of Banang Farm and the villages and little towns from which most of its work force was drawn. The name Banang was derived from one of the local villages where the experimental crop was grown. The centre of attraction whose full name was the Banang Experimental Farm but was popularly referred to only as Banang Farm was by far the largest of the state's Experimental Farms. It comprised sections for agronomy, veterinary science, agricultural engineering and a School of Agriculture, which trained agricultural and veterinary technicians. The farm's produce was sold nationally and overseas. The thousand of people, mainly locals, who worked in Banang, were well paid compared to workers in other places and to them; Banang was the pride of the region. What projected the farm into even greater prominence on this day, a bright Wednesday in the rainy season month of June, was the fact that the country's agriculture minister was paying his first visit, in fact, the very first ever by any agriculture minister to the farm.

The Honourable Mr. Marcus Abongye had been minister for only four months. Prior to that, he was director in charge of professional training in the Ministry of Agriculture. His appointment was a surprise, even to him. What happened was that the government had learnt from intelligence reports that foreign demand for beef, fresh milk, fruits and vegetables was going to rise yearly in the next five years and so in order to cash in on this golden opportunity, it was decided that production of these commodities should be stepped up.

The new minister's appointment came about through the decision that the then agriculture minister, who was an administrator by training and experience, should be replaced by some one who was an experienced agricultural officer with a good first degree in general agriculture and a mater's degree in agricultural administration or education. In the whole country, Marcus Abongye was the only candidate who marched those requirements. And so, he was appointed to the post. Having familiarized himself with the central services of his ministry, he now felt it was time he visited the external services. Considering the importance of Banang Farm, he put it at the top of his agenda. That was why he was expected there on this day.

The minister's motorcade was scheduled to roll into the farm at 11 am. From Dogbe, the provincial head quarters located some ten kilometres from the farm. It was now 10.30pm and the turn-out was already high. Streets had been cleaned and decorated; the main bridge leading into the farm had been painted with the national colours of the country. Over it, a banner read:"Welcome to Banang Farm, Honourable Minister." Officers from the provincial headquarters, political leaders, policemen and gendarmes could be seen looking very busy and some busier than they really were. Some could be heard issuing orders to their subordinates. Locales had lined the streets through which the minister would drive. They looked very happy; for this was the first time they would see a minister at close range.

Among the local people, was one man who looked very nervous. Although he was standing and waiting for the minister like others, he of all people was clearly restless. He kept pacing up and down and halting abruptly and murmuring to himself. However, his neighbours were too busy thinking about and waiting for the minister to notice his state. This was unfortunate as the worrier was one of those standing next to the bridge and could have fretted so much that he could fall into the stream below. All of a sudden, there was some commotion and some one shouted out: "He is here! The minister is coming." Heads turned sharply in the direction from which the minister and his suite were supposed to appear. However, no minister appeared.

"It's a false alert. It's no minister. Can't you see?"

"It's the local police boss coming, no doubt to ensure that all is quiet on the home front. Can't you see that is his car?

Just then, a fairly new Peugeot car with the S.N. initial pulled up to the bridge. A man emerged from the back seat, said a quick hello to the people standing by, crossed the bridge to the other side, bent down and looked at the side, peered into the stream, and went back to the car with a satisfied look on his face. Once he was comfortably seated at the back, he waved to his driver who had waited at the wheel, to take off. Before the car had gone 400 metres, he stopped the driver.

"Wait!" he said as he jumped out of the car. It had suddenly occurred to him that as he inspected the bridge he saw a seriously worried man pacing up and down too close to the bridge. When he returned to the bridge he could not find the man. That made him wander if he had actually spotted such a man or it was only a figment of his imagination

No sooner had the police chief's car disappeared than a siren tore the relative quietness in the air. It was the minister. In a matter of minutes, the entire motorcade had passed and crossed the bridge. Although the minister waved to the crowd from his large black Mercedes car, some people were annoyed at having not shaken hands with him. Of those who felt this way, none did so more than the nervous man who had been restless at the bridge. Peter Akomba as he was called had been the first person to leave home and come and wait for the minister. In fact, he was so early that some people who got to the bridge thinking they would be first but found him already there, joked:

"Peter, how is it that you are here already? Did you spend the night here at the bridge?"

"I have come to see my son. What do you expect?" was his reply as he tried to hide his emotion.

When Peter heard the siren of the minister's security vehicle, his heart jumped. Mechanically, he rushed toward the vehicle. However, since it was a thick crowd the minister's car went pass by the time he turned his way through the crowed. He then tried to run after each subsequent vehicle but was grabbed by the security men.

"Don't! You'll hurt your self."

Another policeman said: "You may get crushed. Be careful"

"Let me go! Let me go! He is my son! Let me go! I want to see him!"

***

The minister visited all the departments of the farm and instructed the staff on what to do. It was such a unique meeting! As he now interacted with them at a different level, memories of childhood flooded his mind. He remembered how some of these so-called officers now running around him, bowing to him and calling him "sir," used to treat the poorer and therefore unfortunate people like him and his mother. He remembered how once when he was sent home from secondary school for fees, his mother, after trying in vain to get his father to pay, had in desperation gone to the home of one of the officers at the farm to plead for assistance. She was received in the kitchen.

"Where? Here, in my house? What makes you think you can just walk into somebody's home and ask her husband to pay your child's fees?" came the man's wife's respond.

"Sorry madam, I am not asking your husband to pay my son's fees. I am asking for a loan which I will pay back. Here he is. You can see for yourself he was driven for fees.

"A loan? But who told you that this was a bank?" retorted the man's wife completely ignoring the bit about the son.

"No, madam, I want…"

"That's enough! You already want money from my husband. That's enough so don't want another thing else!"

At this point, Marcus the minister then aged 12 and in form two, pulled his mother away by the hand:

"Let's go mother, we can't stay here." All this while, the unhelpful wife's husband who was one of the top most officers at the farm had heard every thing from the sitting room where he sat reading a newspaper, but did not utter a word. He did not get up to intervene either. Judging that Rebecca and her son were rather slow in moving themselves from her compound, Mrs. Motanga sent the dogs after them. Mother and child took to their heels. However, for some reason, the two dogs, which were usually ferocious, slowed down and stopped, inexplicably.

At the minister's reception, which was held with pomp and pageantry at the Banang Farm Social Club, destiny chose none other than Mr. Motanga to give the welcome address. Perhaps it was guilt that made him protest when the M.C. for the occasion called on him "to say a word of welcome to his Excellency the minister, on our behalf"

"No! No! Not me but …..

"Come on Mr. Motanga, you are the longest serving senior staff at this farm"

"Well, well it's an honour for me to … to be in this situation. On behalf of every member of this farm and it environs, I wish to extend a hearty welcome to His Excellency, the minister of agriculture Mr. Marcus Abongye.

Since tomorrow is a busy day for the minister, with the working session and audiences, I won't bore him with too much talk. So, welcome Mr. Minister!" There was a thunderous applause. In the mean time as Abongye watched Motanga and listened to him, he wandered if this man remembered those 'atrocities' he committed years ago. Mr. Motanga did not recognize the minister neither did any of those others present, as a child who was born in the farm. Just then, there was some commotion at the door. From what the minister could see, security men were preventing someone from coming into the hall. Hon. Abongye asked his orderly to find out what was going on.

"I have done that already, Your Excellency. It's a man who came without an invitation but wanted to come into the party."

"Why does he want to do that?"

"I don't know, Your Excellency, but he has been saying that he wants to get inside in order to see his son."

Not knowing who he was or which son the man was referring to, the minister took no further notice. As his orderly spoke, a security man pushed the intruder away saying:

"No; you can't come in! You don't have an invitation card!"

"I don't need an invitation card. I have told you the minister is my child."

"How is he your child? If you were the minister's father, would you be out here trying to force your way in instead of being in the hall already? Besides, you are too poorly dressed to be a minister's father. Your shirt is worn out at the neck, your trousers are dirty. In short, you don't look like a minister's father. The minister does not resemble you one bit. So, I don't see the link."

"But I am his father," he said irritated.

"Alright, what is your name?"

"Peter Akomba"

"Akomba? But the minister's name is Abongye. So is he your son?"

"He is my son. It's that he was brought up by his mother. He …" his interlocutor interrupted him with an outburst of mocking laughter.

"Alobana, take him away from here!" He said to a junior officer who stepped forward at once and executed the order.

***

As a matter of fact, Peter Akomba was the minister's father. At the time Marcus Abongye was born, his parents were married for seven years. However the marriage was stormy. Peter came under the intense pressure from his family especially his sisters to send his wife away. The sisters had already found another wife for him. Marcus' parental aunts did every thing to make life unbearable for his mother. At times the aunts would unannounced came from their town which was in another province and live in their brother's house for up to a month during which they would completely ignore Marcus' mother and go about things as if she did not exist. Once, one of Marcus' aunts brought the other wife and provocatively told her in Marcus' mother's presence:

"Eli, why do you sit there idly knowing fully well that your husband will return soon from work and need his food? You know you are the only one he has."

Eli had replied:

"But Ma Bertha doesn't like me. I know I am not his only wife."

"Why did you say that? Are you referring to this thing sitting here?"

Quipped the aunt, disdainfully tilting her head in the direction of Marcus' mother to indicate she was the one she was insulting. Incensed, Marcus' mother swung round: "Don't call me 'this thing'. You know my name. Besides I have had too much trouble from you people, especially you!"

"Then, why don't you leave? Or perhaps you don't know how to go about it. In that that case, I'll show you what to do." Thereupon, Akomba's sister rushed into Marcus' mother's room and promptly re-emerged with her sister-in-law's belongings, which she dumped in the yard. "Take this rubbish with you and go! We don't want you here! Take your hopeless son with you as well. I don't want him to spoil the children of this family."

Rebecca, Marcus' mother in between sobs packed their most essential things in a suitcase, placed it on her head and leading Marcus by the hand, she walked out of the compound. Marcus was then a little boy of seven. His mother took him to her father's compound where she stayed for a year, started dating a new man who was a businessman importing and distributing building materials. Within six months, the man, Paul Abongye, who although thirty but still single, got married to Rebecca. He informally adopted Marcus, regarding and treating him like his own son. He and Rebecca had six other children after Marcus. These were four boys and two girls. Interestingly, all Rebecca's children including Marcus looked like her, which made local observers say things like: "Rebecca's blood is too strong. How can none of her children resemble the father?" two years after Marcus' aunt chased his mother out of their compound, his father had still not bothered to go and see mother and child. Word reaching Rebecca said he now lived happily with the other woman by whom he had a son. In other words, he couldn't care less about Rebecca and Marcus. Four years after, nothing more was heard of Marcus' father.

There was no physical contact between him and Marcus. But once in a while, Marcus would look at some old photographs of the family when his father was still part of it. That was the only kind of physical contact Marcus had with him, if one can call it that.

In all those years, Rebecca with the help of her new husband spared no effort in giving Marcus the best education he could get, both at home and at school. His surname had been changed from Akomba to Abongye. And so, he came to be known as Marcus Abongye. His mother's argument was: "Well, that is as it should be. Why would he bear Akomba when Akomba has never shown that he is his father? Abongye is everything he has."

Unknown to Marcus' biological father, the boy had risen quickly through the academic ranks. When Rebecca took him away from Peter Akomba, the boy was only seven. Because the little boy liked school a lot and his new father enjoyed teaching him at home, he became so good that he skipped some primary classes. When he passed to go to secondary school, his 'father' and mother sent him to the best boarding school in the region. He passed his 'O' Levels with distinction, and did equally well at the 'A' Levels. Since he had shown a keen interest in agriculture, and did very well in the science subjects, his new father insisted he should go to the University of Bogodo and study at the reputed institute of agriculture. He had a BSc. in agriculture and an MSc. In agricultural administration. Upon his return home, he was employed as an agricultural officer in the ministry of agriculture. It was from there that he was appointed agriculture minister. His appointment came as a surprise to him. It came suddenly and unexpectedly one evening during the 5 p.m. radio national news. It was a minor cabinet reshuffle which involved only the agriculture portfolio. This happened through two decrees signed by the head of state himself, with the first retiring the then agriculture minister and the other appointing Marcus Abongye.

All of these developments were unknown to Peter Akomba, Marcus' biological father. In fact, when he heard about Marcus' appointment, it did not strike him that this Marcus Abongye was any one he knew, let alone his own son. At the time, the appointment was read over the radio, Peter was at home playing draughts with a friend. This game had become a favourite pastime of his since he was retired from his job at the farm some five years ago. Within the five years, he had aged rather rapidly and looked frail.

"What was that? A new agriculture minister? What difference does it make? They are all the same, these ministers."

"You can say that again." His friend concurred. Four months later, it was announced that the new minister would be visiting the farm as part of his familiarization tour of the country's external services. A day before the minister visited the farm, a neighbour of Peter Akomba's, burst into his sitting room, out of breath:

"Peter…Peter, do you know who is visiting the Farm tomorrow?"

"It's the new Minister of Agriculture. Isn't it?"

"Yes, but who is he?"

"I don't know. Why should I know anyway?"

"Well, then I'll tell you. It's your own son, I mean it's the boy Marcus, you had with your first wife."

"My little boy, Marcus? But the new minister is called Abongye, not Akomba."

"Well, I can't explain that to you. But you must remember that you abandoned him and his mother. What became of her thereafter or what she did with the little boy, we don't know."

"This is unbelievable! This is unbelievable!" Peter muttered quietly as he slumped into his seat.

That night, he couldn't sleep. His son, a minister? No, there must be a mistake, he thought. He thought of what Marcus must look like so many years after. He recalled with remorse how he had neglected Marcus and how despite putting all his energy into educating the children of his other wife, they had not gone very far academically. Now, he

wished he had looked after his son. He wondered whether
he should go to the reception the following day. Even if he
went, how would he approach Marcus?

"Aren't you sleeping? All you have been doing is turn
yourself round."

"I didn't realize you were awake. I have been thinking."

"About what?"

"The new minister."

"What about him?"

"He is our son."

"What do you mean?"

"He is the son I had with Rebecca."

"No! You are joking! You mean that very big man is *our*
son?"

"Yes, he is."

"Wonders shall never end! But perhaps this is the end of
our troubles. As minister, he is big and rich. So, you needn't
bother about being retired and poor as you are now, as I am
sure he can help us."

"There is no doubt that he can. The question is whether
he will. This is a child I was foolish enough to neglect. Today
he bears another man's name."

"That may be so. But we must bury the past. We must
find a way of convincing him. I suggest that you go and see
him tomorrow. You will have to leave very early before the
whole place becomes crowded."

The following morning, Peter got up early. By the time
he got to the farm, located at about an hours walk, no one
else had arrived. However, within minutes, more people
had started tickling in. At about 8.30 am, which was two
and a half hours after he arrived, there was a crowd,
stretching far from both ends of the bridge where he was
standing to wait for the minister. Groups of people chattered
with one another. Some knew each other, while some were
meeting for the first time. Banang was a large farm with

nine large extensions all of them located in the same area. Since this was all about the minister's visit, people came from all the extensions. Locals who worked for none of the extension also turned out. This greatly increased the number of people who came out to welcome Marcus Abongye.

However, it was also the magnitude of the crowd that prevented Peter Akomba from being noticed by his son Marcus Abongye. Having failed to reach his son at the bridge, Peter Akomba tried again at the reception party that was held in the evening. As we know, he was whisked off by security men. When the three men got Peter out of the club premises, he was let to go home with a warning not to "return and disturb the minister's peace." When Peter got home, he recounted his misfortunes to his wife. After listening to him, she said:

"He is our son and we shall get him. We are going to work out a strategy and get him," she added resolutely. That strategy consisted of Akomba and his wife saving up enough money until one day he travelled to the national capital just to see his long lost son. This was about a year after the minister's visit to the farm.

***

There was a light knock on the door, and then it opened and the minister's secretary came in. Without raising his head from what he was doing, Marcus Abongye asked:

"What's the matter this time Ann?"

"It's a man Your Excellency; he says he must see you."

"Didn't you tell him I was very busy?" he asked, looking up, slightly irritated.

"I did, Your Excellency, but he said it was a matter of life and death."

"Does he have an appointment?"

"No, Your Excellency. He just came in like that."

"What's his name?"

"He wouldn't tell me Your Excellency."

"Okay, show him in."

When Ann opened the door from the minister's adjoining office, Peter Akomba mechanically stood up. He must have thought it was his long lost son. Ann did not notice his nervousness.

"The Minister is ready to see you. Can you come this way, please?"

Peter's heart missed a beat and then fluttered. Peter put his right hand on his heart as if to calm it down. He stood still, closed his eyes and raised his head towards the sky. Not hearing him following her, Ann stopped and turned backwards.

"Are you alright?" she asked, puzzled.

"Yes, yes, I'm fine." He responded. Peter had simply been trying to steady himself for this meeting of a lifetime.

When they got to the door, Ann opened it and stepped aside: "You may go in!"

As soon as Peter stepped into Marcus' office, he found the minister seated. Their eyes met and something moved deep inside both of them. Slowly, Marcus got up, asking:

"Was it you who wanted to see me for a matter of life and death?"

"It's me, Sir."

Marcus looked at him, unable to ask who he was. He just couldn't. This was because some voice within him said this strange man was someone he knew very well. Yet he could not place him. Marcus noticed that he was well dressed. He wore a suit which although not very new, was nevertheless clean. He wore a tie which although incongruous with the other colours he was wearing, was well knotted. Marcus felt this man must be about 60 years of age, possibly retired.

95

"Come and sit down." Marcus said, motioning to one of the guest seats in front of him. Sitting down himself, Marcus inquired:

"What can I do for you?"

Overwhelmed, Peter could not offer a word.

"Can I help you in anyway?" Marcus asked trying to be reassuring.

Pulling himself together, Marcus responded

"I have come to introduce myself to you, your Excellency, I am your father."

"What!" Marcus exclaimed. "My father?"

"Yes Sir, my name is Peter Akomba. I was married to your mother, Rebecca, but the marriage failed and she took you away when you were seven, I think." Peter said, too ashamed to raise his head.

"Are you the father I never had? Are you the father who never cared about my mother or me? You never replied to the letters my mother and I wrote to you. Why have you suddenly appeared now?" Marcus asked in anger.

"I am sorry I treated you and your mother in that way. I'm really sorry. However I must let you get on with your work. I can see I have been a burden." He said as he got up and made for the door.

"No, wait! Wait!" Marcus called out, hurrying to him.

When he got to Peter, he seized him and hugged him. In fact, they hugged each other. As they did so both wept bitterly, the one because of guilt, the other because he was overwhelmed with the emotion of finally connecting with a long lost father.

When they had calmed down, Marcus called his secretary on the intercom phone: "Ann!"

"Yes your Excellency!"

"Get the driver for me!"

Within minutes, the driver came in.

"Fidelis!"

"Your Excellency!"

"I want you to drive my father back to Mabonga. Get ready to leave at once!"

As he realized that his son had finally agreed to accept him, Peter's reaction was:

"Thank you very much, your Excellency! Thank you!"

"Father, don't call me *'Your Excellency'*. You are not my employee."

They both laughed, their eyes still wet. Before Peter left, his son gave him some money.

"This is a lot of money. Thank you very much."

"It's not too much. I believe you have a family, father?"

"Yes, son, I have another wife with children."

Once his father left, Marcus called his secretary.

"Ann, call my mother straight away."

"Alright, Your Excellency."

When his mother came through on the line, Marcus said: "Mother you won't believe this but I met my elusive father today."

"You did? How did that happen?" she said as she sat down.

"He just appeared in the office and introduced himself. What should I do?"

"There is only one thing you can do son. Accept him. Despite what he did, he's still your father. It simply means that you have two fathers. And I am sure your father here would give you the same advice."

"You know what mother? That is exactly how I feel. I was at first very annoyed with him and told him so. However, the feeling of bitterness soon gave way to inexplicably strong feelings of love."

"Those are right feelings my son."

"Mother, I will like to hold a small party at my residence in a month's time. I would like all of us including Pa Peter and his family here in the capital to meet like one family."

"I am all for it my son."

When the conversation was over, Marcus called his wife himself:

"Judith, you know what darling?"

"Not until you tell me."

"I met my long lost father today."

"You did?"

'Yes, he paid me a surprise visit. We were both overwhelmed."

"Was he in good health?"

"He looked alright."

"Judith, I would like us to throw a party in his honour in a month's time. I have already spoken to mum who has given her blessings. It will be one big event bringing together my two fathers. Pa Peter can also bring his family, which is my step mother and children."

"That's fine, darling. I am a hundred percent behind you. Just tell me what you want me to do."

9

Daddy's Boy

It was no secret. Anyone who knew Mr. James and his family was aware that of all his children, he loved David most.

Mr. James as he was widely known in the town was a wealthy business man, in fact the most well-to-do in Tonga town. His real names were James Abanda. However he had come to be known as 'Mr. James' although he should have been called 'Mr. Abanda' or just 'James', as Western etiquette demanded. The explanation is that Tonga town was an African town in an African country and since we Africans show respect to our elders, it was difficult for the people of Tonga town to call James Abanda by his first name. As for the title, 'Mr. Abanda', it must be said that it was used mainly by government officials or businessmen when they were talking business with him.

Mr. James was a man who made his fortune by buying and selling agricultural produce, machinery and fertilizers. He imported them and then sold them to farmers or groups of farmers such as cooperatives. His success was buttressed by the lack of interest other businessmen had in the agricultural sector. He and his family lived well, compared with other members of the Tonga town community.

David was the only boy amongst his children. The first child, Susan Mah, was in the upper sixth in Tonga town most prestigious school, the Government Bilingual School. Pauline Anyim and Benedicta Lum, who were twins, were in the lower sixth of the same institution. Grace Akwen was in Form Four of the reputed girl's school and David himself was just about to go to secondary school. His two younger sisters, Martina Anyoh and Debora Anjim both were in the local government primary school in class seven and five respectively.

However, the spotlight was on David. His father, knowingly or unknowingly made him the centre of attraction. He decided to send him to the most prestigious and the most expensive boarding college in the country. Already, Mr. James was spending a lot of money on David's school items. In fact, he finally spent twice what he spent on the other children when they went to college.

***

When confronted by anybody who dared to ask, Mr. James gave reasons why he loved David so much. Firstly, at the time his wife gave birth to the boy, he had given up on fathering a son. Yet, as he reasoned it, it was very important for him to have a son. His first four children had all been girls. It bothered him that if in the end he did not have a son, there might be no one to succeed him after he had departed from this world. According to the tradition and custom of the Moghamo people, sons, not daughters succeeded men. It was not customary for a man to appoint his nephew or brother or uncle or cousin as successor either. So, it looked as if he was stuck. Although a practising Christian, he contemplated taking a second wife several times just to ensure his succession. This idea gained more and more ground in his mind especially as it troubled him that his wife could no longer give birth. Yet, as far as he knew, she was not on any contraception. Then one day she was pregnant again. Nine months later, David was born. The rest is history.

Mr. James was not stupid. He too had gone to college and had actually done well in his 'O' Levels. It was therefore, no surprise that he passed in ten subjects with good grades – eight 'A's and two 'B's. He was the first of seventeen children in a polygamous family. Just as he was getting ready to go to High School for his 'A' Levels, his father who was a farmer in the village collapsed and died one morning as he walked to the latrine at the back of the house.

As usual tongues wagged about how Mr. James' father had been killed by the dreaded 'Famlah', a secret society to which he allegedly belonged and whose rules he had disregarded. For young James, that sudden death marked the end of his academic pursuits. He could not go to college because there was no one to pay his fees. That was something his father could have done, especially as he had been planning for it. But alas!

While James' mates went on to High school, he found himself looking for a job. He thought of all kinds of possibilities. When his father was alive, his future had looked bright and assured. His mother who was a courageous woman did not waste time musing. She intensified her own petty trading business, which consisted of running a little restaurant, if one can call it that. The restaurant was located in the centre of the town, which constituted the hub of business life. So, it naturally attracted a sizeable number of clients, some of whom were incontrovertible regular customers such as taxi drivers. When her husband died, Mami Mary became very aggressive. She went round business institutions and Government Offices and offered to bring lunch to them in the office. Many of them agreed to place her on trial. And it worked.

Faced with the tragedy of having lost her husband, James' father's other wife realized that if she did not also take steps to look after her own children they would be doomed. This defensive approach adopted by both women drove a wedge between them and in a way pitted the children of one woman against those of the other.

 the

Neither the children nor their mother got any support from any of the young James' paternal family. It was very difficult for James to find a job. However, one evening his mother called him,

"James!"

"Mamma!" he replied as he took a seat in his mother's kitchen.

"Any luck with a job?"

"No, Mamma."

"Don't worry, my son. We shall keep looking. I'm sure that one day, god will provide."

"Yes, Mamma, I won't be discouraged."

"Yes, my son. We have to cope without your father. If he was here, things wouldn't be so difficult for us. But he isn't here."

"Yes, Mamma."

"I spoke to the manager of the Co-operative about you today. He would like you to come and see him tomorrow."

"Okay, Mamma I'll go."

***

The following day, James was at the co-operative before it opened its doors. When the manager got there, he found him waiting but since James knew the manager did not know him in person, he quickly walked up to him and introduced himself. The manager invited him into his office and after they had chatted for some twenty minutes, he informed James that he had decided to engage him as a storeroom assistant. His job would consist of assisting with buying, boxing, storing and distributing farm produce and implements at the co-operative. The salary he was offered was the lowest paid to any employee at the co-operative. But being only a school leaver who had not earned a salary before, James considered his pay package quite handsome. His mother was happy because it was "something coming in," as she put it.

The longer James worked at the co-operative and interacted with his mother, the more he understood about business. After working at the co-operative for three years he told his mother one day that he would like to discuss something with her.

"Yes, my son. What is it?"

"It's my job, Mamma."

"Yes, what about it? I thought you were enjoying it?"

"It's not that. It's that I've been thinking. I have learned a lot about the foodstuff sales business in the three years. I have been at the co-operative. I believe I can now go into business on my own, buying and selling foodstuff and resell in the major cities and even some of the neighbouring countries."

"You are right, James. You are right. But how much do you need to start such a business?"

"Two million francs should be enough. Already I have savings of three hundred thousand francs."

"Alright, I will ask for a loan from the bank."

Within a month, James' mother obtained the loan and he quit the co-operative. He immediately started his own business. And that is how James Abanda became wealthy.

***

Mr. James made a lot of noise about his son going to college

"Have I told you David is going to college?," He would ask a friend or fellow businessman

"No you haven't." would come the reply.

"Of course, he is going to college. I am so pleased. He is going to the great Christ the Lord College."

At home, he was always tilting conversations towards the same topic. If for instance another child said something like:

"Papa, you know I haven't yet bought the things I need to return to college with. So when am I going to have the money so that I can start shopping?"

He would reply;

"What about David? He hasn't finished buying his, has he?"

If his wife mentioned an item for which she needed money from him, he would say: "for God's sake, that can wait! Can't you see I haven't finished with David yet?"

Whenever anything had to be bought for David, his father would create time and go to the market with him. When it was absolutely impossible for him to do so, he would instruct his wife to accompany David, adding:

"And please, select the best items for my son."

"But David is not the only child we have go you know," his wife once pointed out.

"Yes, but he is the only son I have got."

"That doesn't mean we should spoil him."

"I am not spoiling him, I am caring for him."

"Yes, I know, but the other children do not have half the attention you give David."

"But the other children are not sons. David is the only God given son I have. Should I insult God by not handling this gift with care or should I not show the almighty that I appreciate it?

Besides, I am not going to start an argument with you. I don't have time."

On saying those words he stumped out of the bedroom where they were.

***

Two days before the day of David's departure to school, Mr. James rang his house from the office:

"Yes, Abanda's residence. Can I help you? Came the reply at the other end.

"Who is that?"
"It's me papa."
"Who?"
"It's Pauline."
"Where is David?"
"He is here."
"Pass him onto me."
"David."
"Papa!"
"How were you my son?"
"I'm fine, papa!
"Have all your needs been met? Has everything you need been bought?"
"No papa"
"The only thing left is the pullover that is part of the uniform.
"Why has that not been bought?"
"It can only be bought at college when we start."
"Okay, remind me to give enough money to cover that item.

The preferential treatment David got from his father made him behave as if he had a chip on his shoulder. Sometimes he was unnecessarily cheeky to his sisters and would say to them:

"I'll tell papa."

He knew that if he reported any of them to his father, he would reprimand the girls, even if it were him who was wrong. Since the girls did not like being scolded by their father, they usually watched out when David threatened them.

Even David's mother was not spared the consequences of her husband's excessive love for the boy. At times when Mr. James found his wife telling David off for some wrong doing, he would step in:

"What has my son done now? Leave the boy alone! Give him some peace!"

David took advantage of his father's affection and so whenever his mother, for reasons that were entirely for the boy's good, refused to grant him a request, he would go straight to his father who would immediately give him what he wanted.

***

On the night before David left for college, his father held a big feast at his home. Everybody who was anybody in Tonga town was invited and they turned up in large numbers. Some people even came from distant towns and provinces.

There was food in abundance as it was expected for a man of his standing. Mr. James provided a lot of beer, an indispensable delicacy which had long established itself in the country as a status symbol. There was palm wine for those who wanted it. In addition, there was whisky and other spirits. There was also Champagne.

Mr James could be seen excitedly giving orders to other children, his wife, the servants and other relatives who were helping out.

"Give Mr. Zik here a bottle of champagne. He deserves it. Why are those gentle men over there not being served beer? Don't you see the bottles in front of them are empty? Give everyone what he or she wants. Today is a big day in my life. Where is O.C.? O.C. don't you have a drink?"

There was a lot of noise being made. Men scrambled for drinks. Some who had been drinking all evening and had actually hidden bottles of beer in their garments swore that they had not tasted a drop of beer all day. In the lounge where the VIP and elites were sitting, toast after toast was offered to Mr. James and his son. All kinds of flowery expressions were used to describe father and son.

Mr. James was described as "the light of Tonga Town," 'a man of people', 'the richest man in town' and 'he only business man in Tonga Town'. His son was said to be 'the most intelligent boy in the country'. None of these claims were substantiated. But none was challenged either. Outside in the yard different traditional and cultural groups sang, played traditional instruments and danced. At one point, Mr. James went out and ostentatiously stuck bank notes on the faces of the rejoicing people amidst applause. But as was the custom, he waved each note in the air for every one to see before approaching a beneficiary. On such occasions, Mr. James was all smiles.

VIP friends of his who wanted their presence to be felt also rewarded the dancers, singers and players in like manner.

At one point, Mr. James got up and clapped his hands while clearing his throat. This was a sign that he wanted to make a speech. Everyone in the room fell silent. Only the sound of festivity out in the yard broke the silence. Promptly, someone from inside stepped out and shouted above the noise:

"Be quiet everybody! The big man is about to speak to us."

There was total silence. Mr. James cleared his throat and began:

"VIPs, distinguished guests, ladies and gentlemen welcome to my residence. My family and I are very pleased to have you here this evening. Just in case anybody is unsure, the reason why we are here is to honour my beloved son whom as you know is going to college. David has worked very hard both at school and at home. His teachers have spoken very well about him. I'm sure that he will do equally well at Christ the Lord's College. I'm prepared to do everything possible for my son so that he can have the education I never had. Where is David?"

"Here I am, papa." The boy answered as he came in from outside.

"Come and stand next to me, my son. Ladies and gentlemen, this is the hero of this occasion." There was a round of applause with some guests actually standing up to give David a standing ovation. His father spoke again:

"Thank you ladies and gentlemen! Thank you very much! Thank you! Thank you! Please, eat and drink as much as you like. This is a big day for us, so you must enjoy yourselves. In fact, there is enough to eat and drink until tomorrow morning and beyond. Thank you very much!"

The guests took this invitation seriously and by five o'clock the following morning, some people were so drunk they had fallen to the ground and gone to sleep. The stronger ones were still awake and were either chattering like magpies, or were singing or leaning over backwards or forwards in their seats and snoring. Those with some self control had managed to return home.

Mr. James' compound on that morning was in a sorry state. Litter was strewn all over the place. There were empty bottles of beer that had fallen over, some broken; unfinished food in disposable plates, cutlery and drinking glasses. Mr. James was the first person to get up that morning.

"Judith! Judith!" he called as he stepped into the lounge.

"Here I am!" his wife responded coming from behind him.

"But what is happening? Are these things not going to be cleared up? Have you forgotten David is leaving today?"

At once Mr. James' wife turned to the girls"

"Girls, come out so that we can tidy up the house."

***

David's school, according to information contained in his prospectus was scheduled to re-open on the 14th of September just like other colleges, and indeed even primary schools throughout the country. Students of Christ the Lord's College were expected to report to their dormitories at 4.p.m.

Mr. James left his office much earlier than usual. In fact, he was back home by 1.p.m. and could be seen and heard giving instructions:

"Judith, have David's things been properly packed? Where is the driver? Can someone ask him to get ready because we are leaving for college at exactly 3 o'clock?"

***

When Mr. James' car entered the school gate, David was struck at how beautiful the compound was. The houses on the right which he later understood were staff houses were very different in structure from any other residential houses he had seen. These ones were designed and executed in a style that stood out. Not even his father's houses, the one in which they lived Ngomgham quarter or the others dotted here and there in some of the country's major towns and being rented by the state or individuals were as good as the ones he was seeing. In fact, he was soon to realize that all the houses in the college were built in the same style. The only thing he had seen that had any resemblance to the houses at his new school, were the ones in photographs his father had taken on a business trip to Europe. David's father who had been to Europe only that once fetched those photographs, once in a while to muse over them for the sake of nostalgia. At such times, he would say things like:

"Oh! When I was in Europe! You see, I went to Paris, Bonn and London. Don't you see, these houses are on the out skirt of London, Elstree and Borehamwood, to be more precise, I took them with my camera when I was travelling up north to Manchester. My dream is for my son to eventually go to Britain and stay there to study. My son will go!"

As the car advanced towards the main blocks of the campus, David continued to be struck. He saw three large football fields next to each other, until now, he had only seen a single football pitch in each educational institution. It must however be said that Tonga was the only town he knew. For some reason that was never explained, his beloved father never gave him the opportunity to travel out of the town. Once one of David's maternal uncles invited him to spend the holidays with him in the economic capital of the country, Mr. James promptly said:

"Dear Paul, thank you for asking me to send David to you for the holidays. However, I prefer to have my son with me."

On Mr. James' instructions, the driver drove to the principal's house. On hearing the sound of a car pulling up outside, Fr. Patrick went to the window, pulled the blinds to one side and looked out. He recognized Mr. James as he had seen him a couple of times before, the last occasion being when he came to pay his son's deposit for admission. He opened the door. Mr. James could tell by the look in the priest's face that he did not like this impromptu visit.

"Sorry Father! Sorry to disturb you."

"It's alright Mr. James. What can I do for you?"

"It's the boy. I brought the boy." He said excitedly

"I'm afraid I don't understand. What boy are you talking about?" responded the principal in that straight forward manner. That is so typical of the British.

"My son, Father. David, It's David, your student."

"Oh yes of course. But you shouldn't bring him to me, worse still my house. New students are to be handed to Form Five prefects in the form one dormitory. That is where you should take him. It's clearly spelt out in the prospectus of which I believe you have a copy.

"I know that, father. But I wanted to hand him personally to you."

"Why? Arrangements have been made for the new children to be looked after. I have some five hundred children here. Can you imagine what the situation would be like if every parent had to bring his or her child to me in the house on the first day of term?"

"I also would like to finish paying my son's school fee."

"How much do you want to pay?"

"The balance for the year."

"That's very good, Mr James. I wish we had more parents like you. Most parents want to pay in instalments. In that case, let's go to my office."

At the principal's office, Mr. James paid the entire amount outstanding. The total amount paid for the academic year was one hundred and fifty thousand francs.

"Can I also leave his pocket allowance with you, Father?"

"Of course, you can. Other parents do that. How much were you thinking of leaving for him?"

"Fifty thousand Francs."

"Fifty? Is that for the whole year?"

"No, for the first term."

"But fifty thousand francs is too much, Mr. James. This is a boarding school, which means your son will be housed and fed by the college. So, what does he need all that money for? If you ask me, I will say the maximum he should have is thirty thousand francs on the basis of ten thousand francs a month."

"It's just that I want the boy to be fine at school."

"Of course, he will be fine. I'm sure that you have bought his basic needs like toiletries, shoes and clothing. Haven't you?"

"Yes, I have, Father."

"So, why would he still need that kind of money? Why?"

"It's because I don't want him to suffer the way I did, Father. You don't know the kind of terrible childhood I had."

"I can understand that. But why would David suffer when you have made provision for all his needs here at school? I really don't think you should spoil him. Instead, train him to understand that life is not a bed of roses and that one has to work hard to get what one wants."

"You are right, Father. But it's just that it's hard when I remember what I went through. Besides, he is my only boy."

"I understand you, Mr. James. But I too had a difficult childhood. I lost my father when I was only seven. He was a miner in Scotland. He had catered for the family since my mother who came from the Republic of Ireland, from Dublin precisely, was unemployed. When my father died, life became even more difficult. A year later, my mother too died. I was then raised by my maternal grandparents who actually brought me up along with their own eight children. Fortunately for them, and I suppose for me, my parents only had me. When I was fifteen and in the fifth form of a catholic college in Glasgow, my grandfather died. His death was a heavy blow for my grandmother since it was her husband who was the breadwinner. At that stage, the priests who ran our college decided to be my guardians. By the time I had my Advanced Levels? I had already made up my mind about joining the priesthood. This stemmed from the profound admiration I had for Fathers Abraham and Raymond. I was touched deeply whenever I considered that people like them had put their lives and future at the service of God and mankind. Without them, would I have become what I am today? Would I? M. James, answer me."

"I don't think so, Father."

"So I don't think that you alone can give your child everything he needs. Do you what plans God has for him or even for you?"

"No, I don't, to be honest with you."

"And when you tell me David is your only son, I don't understand. Does it matter that he is your only son? A child is a child. They are all given by God. How many girls have you got, by the way?"

"I have six."

"So you have seven children. Yet you speak of the boy as if he was your only child. Do the girls not matter? Anyway, how much money have you decided to leave for the boy?"

"I think I'll take your advice and leave thirty thousand francs."

"That's wonderful. And I'm sure that's the right decision. But where's the boy? I should like to see him."

"He is in the car. He is with the driver. David! David!" Mr James called out after stepping our of the principal's office. David heard, and so, got out of the car and ran up the stairs from the assembly ground.

"So this is your little boy?" Father asked Mr James while offering David a handshake.

"Yes, this is my boy."

"What's your name, young man?"

"David, sir." He answered feeling a bit tense.

"How are you, David?," asked the principal, trying to sound reassuring.

"I'm fine, sir."

"No, you say, 'Father' to me, not 'sir'. I am a priest."

"I am sorry, sir; I mean, Father."

"There's no need to be apologetic. Just remember that. How old are you, boy?"

"Eleven, Father."

"Listen to me, David. Your father has just paid you fee for the whole term. He has also left some pocket money here for you. I will keep it and give it to you when I feel you need it. One thing I want you to know is that you are a very lucky boy. Your father loves you and cared for you. However, I want you to know that the world is a place where people must learn to do things for themselves. Here at the Christ the Lord College, we hold strongly to those principles. That is a philosophy you must learn. Well, Mr James, I'll get some senior students to direct your driver to the Form One dormitories. There you will find Form Five prefects ready to receive your son."

When the car pulled up at St. Jude's dormitory, two boys, evidently bigger and older than David, went up to the car. One of them spoke to David's father.

"Good afternoon, sir. Are you a new parent?"

"A new parent?"

E"I mean, are you the parent of a new student?"

"Oh yes! I m the father of David here. He is new first year student."

"I see. We are final year students and prefects. We are the ones who receive new students. Is that David?" he asked, pointing to Mr. James' boy, sitting at the back of the Peugeot 505.

"Yes, that's him. That's David." He answered, beckoning to the boy to come and join him.

When David went over to them, his father continues: "David, these are senior students who are here to receive you new boys."

"Hello, David! My name is Christopher. That is Gabriel and next to him is Mathias. We are prefects in charge of the two form one dormitories. Are your things in the car? I mean apart from the mattress which is tied to the roof of the car."

"Yes, I have my suitcase and other things in the boot."

"You must be careful, by the way. In this school junior students address the senior ones as "Monsieur." Turning to David's father, Christopher said:

"Please sir, if you can ask the driver to get David's things out of the car, then we can take them into the dormitory. Let me get the mattress from the roof of the car."

When they entered the dormitory, David was amazed to see so many beds in one house. He saw boys about his age being very busy, chatting in groups and going about together as if they had known each other before. As his father

114

removed his things from his large and expensive suitcase, and he looked around, bewildered, he also noticed other boys seated on their beds, some of them passing by, and yet others standing at a distance. They were looking in his direction. However, he did not know what exactly was interesting them.

What caught his attention most was a number of students – five – who were mopping up a part of the dormitory that had little pools of standing water. In fact, this was the part of the dormitory where the form five prefects who had brought his and his father to the dormitory had selected a bed for David. The problem was that the many new students who had arrived at the school before David - and some were already there in the morning - had carefully chosen beds in the other dormitory where there was no standing water on the floor.

David wondered with worry if he too would have to clean up the floor. He secretly hoped that his father would stay with him until the dirty work had been done. He knew that if his father stayed longer the tall and big boys would not dare to ask him to clean the floor. Even if they did, his father would not allow him do it.

Unfortunately for David, when the driver had finished making the bed, his father thanked the prefects and suddenly announced: "Right, David my son, I go now. I know you are in good hands." Without waiting for his son to respond, Mr. James pressed a bank note into his hand and added: "Take that, just in case you need it. As you know, I left your pocket money with the principal."

Turning to the driver, he said:

"Come and let's go!"

As soon as David's father left the dormitory, one of the bigger boys, as if he had been waiting for the opportunity, went over to Christopher who was talking to David and said:

"*Boh,* do you know that fox?"

"No, Eddie. I've just met him and his father today."

"The fox looks quite rich. He even has a tailor-made cotton mattress and a pillow to match…Fox, what's your name?"

Lost, David kept quiet.

"What's your name?" he thundered.

"Say your name!" Christopher urged.

"But I am not a fox. I am not an animal."

"You are a fox. If you didn't know that, I want you to know it now. I am the dormitory captain here and I make the rules." Turning to Christopher, the dormitory captain said:

"*Boh,* what have you been doing with this fox if you haven't told him who he is?"

"You tell him, Boh. After all, he is in your dormitory. I am only a visitor here, you know? Anyway, I'll leave you now, David. Bye."

"So that's the little name, eh? Come here, you little devil!" David barked, pulling David's ear.

"I didn't. I…"

"Shut up, you fox! Kneel down here!" he ordered as he pressed David down to the kneeling position. Tears started rolling down his eyes.

"Are you crying already? I haven't beaten you yet, you know? I also beat little boys like you. Remain kneeling until I return. Upon saying that, David left the dormitory.

David hoped that one of the other three form five students who sere in the dormitory would come to his aid. None did. They just went about their own matters as if he did not exist. The truth is that there was solidarity among form five students of the school and it would have been very difficult for any classmate to contradict Eddie by asking David to stand up.

However, feeling great numbness in his knees, David raised himself. Promptly, another boy his age who had been watching him with sympathy rushed towards David:

"Don't! Don't get up! You will get in greater trouble if you do. You don't know Monsieur Eddie."

David knelt back.

A few minutes later, the dormitory captain returned and said to David as he sat on his bed in one of the corners of the dormitory:

"Come here, Fox!"

David got up and went to Eddie.

"So what's your name?"

"David."

"Answer me; 'Monsieur'"

"I mean, David, Monsieur."

"Good. David who? What's your family name?"

"Abanda? You mean you are related to the big businessman in town? Was that him who was here?"

"Yes, Monsieur."

"Then you must be very rich."

David said nothing.

"You are the only boy in this dormitory with a cotton mattress. Most of us have grass mattresses. Some students even have ordinary mats. What have you got in your box?"

"My things, Monsieur."

"What things? Go and open it so that I can see for myself."

***

When David opened his box, Monsieur Eddie was amazed by what was it. Some of the things were ordinary items such as toiletries but the quality of David's was very superior and obviously a lot more expensive. The quantity of items was equally astonishing.

"I'll select mine," the dormitory captain said as he bent over the box with its lid thrown open on David' bed and picked up two tablets of soap, a packet of biscuits, two ball point pens, a pair of socks and a can of deodorant. As he turned round to walk away, David protested:

"Those are my things. Why are you taking them away?"

"Shut up! I take what I like around here. I am the dormitory captain."

Having said that, he walked back into his 'space'. David was in tears.

Just then, David heard a distant hand bell. One of the big boys announced:

"Form One boys, that's the bell for supper. Get your complete sets of cutlery and go to the refectory. If you don't know the way, follow those who do."

As David joined the crowd, he felt a pat on his shoulder. Turning round, he found it was the boy who had advised him not to get up when the dormitory captain asked him to kneel for punishment."

"What's your name?" he asked David as they climbed the stairs that led away from the form one dormitories to the games room and then St. John's dormitory and finally the refectory.

"David. And what's yours?"

"Cuthbert."

"Cuth what?"

"Cuthbert. Don't you know the name?"

"No, I have not heard it before."

"Yes, I know. People have told me that a lot of times."

***

When the boys got to the refectory, they found that there were bigger and older boys standing outside of the building and showing them the part of the refectory to which to go.

"Form One boys, go to the Form One compartment! Just go in through that door and you will find someone to assign you to a seat."

Once inside the refectory, David, his new friend Cuthbert and some ten other new boys were shown a table at which they sat. When all the new boys had been made to sit down, an older boy who said he was in Form Two addressed the new boys. He welcomed them and told them that there was a Form Two boy like him on each Form One table. He said his name was Gregory and then issued a warning:

"Be quiet! Some of you are talking when I al talking. You may get severely punished for that. So, you better be quiet!"

There was silence. So, he went on: "Can you all put your cutlery on the table, just in front of you? Do that before I start...No talking, please! I didn't ask you to talk. You that boy with a gateau head, stand up! Yes? You! What's your name?"

"David."

"David who?"

"Abanda."

"Okay, remain standing!"

"But I didn't do anything."

"Don't argue with me, you fox!"

David stood as ordered. But he felt embarrassed because in the whole large refectory of five compartments and thirty tables, which amounted to some 530 students, he was the only one standing because he was being punished. A lot of other students looked at him. So he felt humiliated. He thought about his father.

"As I was saying before I was rudely interrupted," Gregory went on, "put your cutlery on the table and make sure your knife and fork are on either side of your plate of rice. Place the knife on the right and the fork on the left. Do that quickly because in a few minutes we are going to pray. Sit down now, David, and be very careful next time."

Just then, a bell sounded somewhere in the refectory and silence descended upon the house which only a few minutes was humming like a swarm of bees as different people talked at different tables.

David noted that in the middle compartment someone was standing on a raised platform with a bell in his hand. David was soon to realize that this senior student would use the platform very often. He learned he was the refectorian.

"Can you stand up for prayers, please?"

Everyone rose and refectorian prayed. As soon as prayer was over, everyone sat down and immediately started eating.

Gregory reminded the new students at his table of good table manners:

"Hold your fork in the left hand and your knife in the right hand. Eat gently, don't rush. You are not fighting and it's not a race. Don't open your mouth while chewing, don't drop food on the table and make sure that you leave particles of food in your plate when you have finished."

Throughout the meal, Gregory kept a watchful eye on his boys. It was interesting to see most of them struggling with their knives and forks. Even David did not find the exercise easy. Although his father was wealthy, neither he nor his wife ever insisted on the children using their cutlery correctly. The next few weeks therefore continued to be very trying ones.

After nearly all the students had finished eating, a number of prefects, including the refectorian, made announcements. The refectorian instructed the new students to take their plates to their dormitories and wash them for breakfast the following morning. After each meal, he said, they would treat the plates in the same way.

The senior prefect welcomed Form On students and any other students coming to the college for the first time. He then said:

"The time now is half past six. You have an hour during which you can rest, walk around the school, stay in the dormitory and chat with your friends. But you must not stay here in the refectory because it has to be cleaned up. For the Form One students, if there are still any of you who do not yet know which is their classroom, you will find the list of students assigned to each of the two Form One classrooms pinned on each of the doors. However, I have copies of the lists which I will now read out to you."

He read out the names and it turned out that both David and his new friend, Cuthbert, were in the same class, 1A. David's friend nudged him and said excitedly:

"We are in the same class. Have you found a desk for yourself?"

"No, I haven't. I don't even know where the classrooms are."

"I know where they are. I'll take you there. Come on, let's go!"

"The bugle sounded and David, Cuthbert and two or three other boys who sat on the stairs leading to the main entrance of the main building woke up with a start.

"What is that?" David asked Daniel, a second year student who had been telling them about life at the college.

"Oh, that? It's the bugle."

"What's a bugle?" the boys asked in chorus.

"A bugle is like a trumpet. It is used mainly in military camps to rally soldiers; here at our college, it is used because the compound is large and the refectory bell would not be loud enough. You will be hearing the bugle twice everyday, once early in the morning to wake you up and at half past seven at night to remind you that it's time to go to class for prep. Well, you should be hurrying to your classrooms now. Go on!"

When David and his friends entered the main block, he noticed there were very many students going in different directions. Some were going upstairs and others were going to the classrooms downstairs. David's classroom was one of the downstairs ones. When he got to the classroom he found there were some students already at their desks. He and Cuthbert went to their seats.

When all the students of Form 1A had come in and taken their seats, the Form Five prefect who was at the teacher's seat addressed them:

"Good evening, everyone!"

"Good evening!" came the collective response.

"No, that's not good enough. You must answer me by saying "good evening, Monsieur." I am sure you have been told that already. This classroom. Unlike in the primary school where you had one classroom with one teacher teaching all subjects, here you will have different teachers teaching different subjects to you in the same classroom.

"During lesson time the subject teacher will be in charge of you. In the dormitory you will be looked after by your dormitory captain, when you are here for prep, I will be in charge of you. I expect you to be well behaved and to do as you are told. Any disobedience will be severely punished. And by the way, any prefect has the right to give you instructions and punish you. Now I will take the register to see those who are present and those who are absent. Before I do that, has anyone any questions?"

One hand went up.

"We don't know your name!"

"Okay, I'll tell you what it is. It's Theophille. But you can call me, Monsieur Theo."

Having said that, the prefect started marking the register. When he got to David's name, he said:

"David Abanda? Where are you? Are you related to the business tycoon, James Abanda?"

"He is my father." Came David's answer.

As soon as David said that, heads turned towards him. "Your father is very well known. He is also one of the richest men in town, if not the richest. But I must warn you that your father's name will not stop you from being punished if you break school rules."

When David and others returned to the dormitory, he and Cuthbert walked to his bed and sat on it. There was no problem with that as other children were mixing freely with their mates. As the new boys were soon going to find out, this period between prep and lights out which was from 9 O'clock to 10 O'clock was what might be called a free period.

One by one, students went up to David's bed. They asked him questions.

"I heard Monsieur Theo talking about your father. Is he really rich and famous?"

"Well, that's what people say."

Another boy asked him what life was like in such a wealthy family. Others felt his mattress and pillow and commented that they were both very soft.

"What's inside? Surely, it's not grass."

"No, it's cotton. My father had them specially made for me."

"You are lucky. You are the only boy in this dormitory with a specially made cotton mattress. Not even the Form Five prefects have it. Most people have grass mattresses. As you can see… I have a mat, not a mattress, let alone a cotton one."

As they discussed, a group of three older boys entered the dormitory. The manner in which they interacted with the Form Five boys in the dormitory left none of the new boys that they too were Form Five students.

"Where is that rich boy? We hear there is a rich boy in this dormitory. Where is he? Ah! Is it you? I think it is. What is your name?" One of the big boys said, pointing to David.

"My name is David."

"David who?"

"Abanda. David Abanda."

"Yes, it's him. You are the son of the rich businessman. Tell me, how rich are you?"

"I'm not rich, Monsieur."

"Don't lie to me, you fox! You are rich! You must be. You are the son of Abanda." Turning to his two companions, the speaker said:

"Guys, let's go! We know where to find him." They said good night to the other Form Fives and left. About ten minutes later, the power house gave the lights out warning. At once the dormitory captain announced:

"To bed, everybody! No more movements!"

Five minutes later, the lights went out definitely. As David lay in bed on that first night at college, a thousand and one thoughts flooded into his head. After from the few moments of joy such as when he met his new friend, Cuthbert, David felt Day 1 at college had been uninspiring. He felt that if really and truly this was what college life was all about, then he was in for a tough time. However, he felt consoled when he remembered that his father had told him if anyone gave him trouble at school, he should inform him at once.

Some boys were already snoring. With exception of the Form Five students who were talking quietly in low tone in the light of the bush lamps they had lit in their 'spaces', every other boy was firmly ensconced in bed. David turned over and lay on his belly, his right leg pulled up slightly and his arms held together so that his head rested on them. This was his favourite sleeping position. His eyes were already beginning to be heavy with sleep. He yawned a couple of times.

Now he was half asleep and half awake. Slowly, he slid into slumber land…The next minute he found himself sitting next to his father as they drove around town. David told him about the hard times he was facing at school.

"Does the principal know about this?" he asked his son.

"No, dad. I can't tell him."

"Why not?"

"Because the prefect will punish me if I do."

"Then I will come and talk to the principal one of these days."

***

The following day, classes started in full swing. David found himself being introduced to new subjects such as biology, physics, chemistry and laboratory work. He was not too surprised by the familiar subjects such as history geography, English and religious studies. He was glad to find that French which he started in primary school was very much part of the curriculum. His new French teacher, a certain Monsieur Ngatchou repeatedly urged them to take the subject seriously because as he told them: "You will need French in future on a daily basis. Remember that it is one of our country's official languages."

What struck David the most was that early every teacher who came to the classroom and heard or saw the name 'Abanda', immediately asked him something like: "Do you know Mr. James Abanda?," or "Are you related to the businessman Abanda?" or even, "Are you the son of Mr. James the business tycoon?" Before long, the entire staff body had known that the business magnet James Abanda had a son at the college. Among the students, the news spread like wild fire.

David was a student in a class of his own. He was one of the very ones who had bought every item mentioned in the prospectus. He even went as far as procuring all of his classroom needs. In fact, where the prospectus required a single item, David's father bought more – sometimes up to five. When his wife pointed out that he was too soft with the boy, he responded.

"I don't want my boy to lack anything. He is my only boy, you know?" As if that was not enough, for each item Mr James bought, he went for the best and most expensive.

As a result, in the whole school, David had the most expensive shoes, shirts, trousers, socks, pens, books and cutlery. He even had four brand new suits with ties to match.

Before David's first week at college ended, every student had known him. Some of them; especially the Form Fives began to get closer to him. Some went to his dormitory just to visit him. Even so, that would not have been a problem had some of the students not pushed it too far.

When they went to see him they would say things like: "Dave? Do you have any more garri? Can I have a little with some sugar?" Others went to see him for biscuits, shoe polish and tooth paste. The older ones borrowed items of clothing from him and the more ruthless ones obtained loans of money. Of course, not all the borrowed items were ever returned.

David was not an arrogant boy. Nevertheless, if he felt betrayed or unfairly hurt, he could fight for his rights. That was exactly what happened when one day Cuthbert told him a second year boy had said all that wealth his father had came from money his father had "stole." Cuthbert gave his friend the information one day when they were walking to the dormitory after lunch.

"What! Did he say that about my father? "David screamed

"Yes, he said it to me."

"I'll teach him a lesson! Just wait until I find him!"

Just as David was saying this, he saw Edward, the second year boy in question walking towards him and Cuthbert. Edward was with two other second year students. When Edward saw David advancing towards them, he said something to his two companions, pointed at David and all of them second years, laughed mockingly.

David rushed up to Edward, caught hold of his shirt collar and challenged him:

"Repeat to me what you said about my father"

"Hey! What does this fox think he is doing? Let go of my shirt! Let go or you'll be sorry for yourself!"

"Sorry for myself? Are you kidding? I will teach you a lesson. How dare you insult my father?"

The other two second year students grabbed hold of David and invited Edward to punch him. Edward did and David screamed loudly. When the boys released David, he was in such great pain that he dropped to the ground, moaning. Cuthbert ran off for help.

The following day after lunch, the senior prefect sent for David. By the time he got to his office Edward and his two mates were already there. A few minutes later, Cuthbert came in. After listening to all five boys, the S.P. ruled that Edward was wrong. He also stated that David had acted in self defence. Edward was made to apologize and David promised never to behave in that manner again.

Within a week, David's father learned about the incident. It was not his son who reported it to him. The boy could not say who had told his father. Mr. James drove straight to the college and at once confronted the principal. He was so agitated that when he knocked at the principal's office, he did not wait for a reply before going in.

"But Mr. Abanda that is no way to enter an office!"

"But I knocked, Mr Principal. However, that is not why I am here. Can you tell me what is going on here with my son?"

"Your son? Is there anything wrong with him?"

"Don't tell you don't know, Mr. Principal! My child is being ill-treated at this school and you know it!"

"I'm afraid I don't know what you're talking about. In any case, I can assure you that your child is in the capable hands of our prefects here."

"But they beat him!"

"There's nothing to worry about, Mr Abanda. If there was anything unusual going on, I would have known about it. Take my word for it."

"No, I can't. My son is badly treated here and I want those boys who have been harassing him to be punished!

By this time, David's father was shouting at the principal. Angered, the principal rose violently and retorted:

"Listen to me, Mr Abanda. I will not let the likes of you come here and tell me how to run my school!"

"I am not telling you how to run your school. I am asking you to do the things you ought to be doing."

Some children, who had been playing on the assembly ground, heard the angry voices. They Stopped and listen. They recognized the principal's voice but were not too sure who the other person was. That quarrel struck them. Although they had seen the principal getting angry with students, this was the first time he had lost his temper with an adult to the extent of quarrelling. The boys were separated from the principal's office by a flight of some thirty steps and a veranda.

Because the thirty steps were high enough for the principal not to spot the eavesdroppers on the playground, they stayed there and continued to listen to the quarrel.

The next thing they heard was the principal saying to this guest: "I have had enough of this. And now if you don't mind, I'd like to be left alone so that I can get on with my work."

"Okay, I have now become a man who comes here to disturb you. Mr. Principal, I don't think you know who I am yet."

"Of course, I do, Mr. Abanda. You are one of our parents."

"Mr. Principal, I'm not just a parent here. I am an important man in this town! I'm a V.I.P.!"

"But, Mr. Abanda, all our parents are equal before or eyes. The only V.I.P. here is the almighty God!

"Oh, yes! But I paid my child's fees here for the whole year. How many other parents did?"

As soon as he said that, he walked out of the principal's office, slammed the door behind him and ran down the stairs. Once he entered the car, he drove himself out of the campus, ignoring the driver whom he made to take the passenger seat. So upset was he that by the time he remembered he should have asked to see his son, at least to say hello to hi,; he was far away from the school. Nonetheless, the next day, he returned to the college, apologized to the principal and asked to se David. Father sent for his son whom he embraced several times. David's father informed him he had discussed with the principal the treatment he was being given by the older boys. He did not go into any details. His son also did not ask questions. What preoccupied him was the fear of reprisals by the bullies. Unknown to him at the time, the said boys were not going to harden their hearts towards him. Although he never said so, he suspected the principal must have reprimanded them, or even punished them. But did that mean his father had named them to the principal, he wondered? How could he when David never told him who the boys were?

Before Mr. James left his son, he gave him a number of items he brought for him, including two brand new suits, again complete with shirts and ties to match, shoes, biscuits, garri, jam, peanut butter and a relatively substantial amount of money. He asked the boy not to let the principal know that he had given him money directly.

By the time the third term began, David had more or less, settled in. Like the other children, he went about his everyday tasks normally. However, he continued to be the centre of attraction. He had also steeled himself against the taunts of other students. Nevertheless, in no way was this boy born with a silver spoon in his mouth, ready for what was soon to happen to him.

On Tuesday morning while David was in his geography lesson, the school clerk, Mr. Kusia, knocked at the door. The teacher went to the door and spoke with the clerk in low tones, and then he went outside and closed the door behind him so that he and the clerk were now outside and alone. The students murmured. Hearing this, the teacher opened the door and warned them to be quiet. The reason why the class had become agitated was that geography was a lesson they enjoyed very much and so were not happy that the lesson was interrupted. This was especially true on this day because the teacher, Mr. Nkims, had just started a thrilling topic called "the stages of a river."

While Mr. Kusia waited outside, Mr. Nkims opened the door and called out David. When the student got outside, his classmates noticed that he was being taken away by the school clerk. Back in the classroom, the teacher said to them: "Alright, let's get on with the lesson!" at once they pulled themselves together. What they did not know was that the clerk had just said to David: "David, the principal wants you." As the young student walked to the principal's office, he wondered why the principal would want him.

"Come in, David! And sit down! », the principal said to him.

As soon as the boy sat down, the principal who looked worried, told him: "David, I'm sorry to inform you that your father has died. I'm told he died last night in a car crash."

David was lost. He heard the principal quite alright, but somehow, he was overpowered by too many thoughts and emotions. He felt hot inside of himself. His head felt as if it was expanding from inside, his heart pounded, then fluttered as if it was contracting. He himself felt some sweat trickling down his face and neck. Before he realized it, he was weeping and shouting "No! No! No!"

The principal tapped him on the back and said: "I'm sorry, David. I know how you feel."

Just ten, a taxi pulled up outside and out of it came David's mother, weeping loudly. As soon as David saw her, he ran out of the principal's office and down the stairs. Mother and child hugged each other and sobbed very loudly. Students in top floor classrooms of the main building peered down from the windows, but suddenly they all disappeared. They must have been ordered back to their seats by their teachers.

The principal was very understanding. He authorized David's mother to accompany her son to the dormitory, pick up some of his belongings and take him home for his father's funeral.

"How did it happen, mum?" David asked as they walked down to the dormitory.

"I don't know, son. It was late last night when a telephone call came from the police station saying your father had been involved din a car crash and was at the General Hospital. When I got to the hospital, your father was unconscious. He died two hours after I arrived at the hospital."

"Did he say what happened?"

"No, he didn't say anything at all. He couldn't speak."

"Where was he when the accident happened?"

"He was going to a business meeting. According to what the police said, his car and a truck ran into each other near the main market."

"Was it you who told the principal?"

"No, it wasn't. It must have been the police."

When David and his mother got home, they found some of David's paternal uncles carrying away some of his father's things. His mother was shocked at that.

"What are you people doing?" she screamed.

"We are taking away our brother's things. We have to look after his things, now that he is no more."

"Why do you speak as though there is no one left in his house?"

"I know you are here." Said one of David's uncles. "But you are a woman. Can you wear the suits and shoes he left?"

"Oh no! This is a disgrace! You hear your brother has died. You haven't even seen the corpse, yet you are fighting over his property?"

But the men were not listening. They had returned to their booty.

From that day, school life for David went down hill. After his father's burial, he returned to school. He had been away for three weeks. End of year exams started a week later but the young man was clearly not in the mood for such an exercise. He was still shocked and traumatized. As might be expected, he failed his exams and was ear-marked to repeat Form One.

Worse was to come, for at the beginning of the new school year, he could not even return to school, for want of money. His mother, now his sole guardian on earth, did not have enough money to send him back to school. Two factors accounted for this state of affairs. Firstly, David's uncles had confiscated his father's banking documents, including his cheque books. Secondly, his father had not left a will. In his company, employees were in disarray. None of them received any salary as nobody seemed to know what to do. Mr. Abanda had not made any contingency plans in case he was not on the scene.

Life became tough for David's mother who now found herself in the unenviable situation of fending for her children single-handed. She felt angry at the way her in-laws treated her and the children of their own brother. She felt hurt when she thought she was now in this mess just because her husband had neglected taking precautions to protect his family. She contemplated taking her husband's brothers to court but dropped the matter when lawyers advised her about how much she would have to pay for the service.

When the new school year began, David's mother still did not have enough money to send him - or his sister Grace who was at the Holy Mother College — back to school. A good idea came to her and she acted on it. She moved both children to the Government High School where her other children, Susana, Pauline and Benedicta were. She then started a home restaurant business. This consisted of selling different national dishes and other delicacies at home. It was only in this way that she was able to continue to educate her children.

Nevertheless, for David, this was a big disappointment, for the Government High School was in no way comparable to his former school. The latter was after all the best in the country! The new school was a crowded, poorly planned and badly built institution with no boarding facilities. Frankly, from then on, for David, life became an uphill struggle. Even he knew that nothing would ever be the same again.

10

Chicken Soup

Infants 1A were released for Long Break first. As soon as the bell went, Ni Martin rushed next door to see if our class, 1B, was out already. As the door to our class was still locked, he concluded that we still in the classroom. So, he came over to the set of glass windows that stood on two of our classroom walls and pressed his face against the pane. His eyes caught those of Madam as she paced up and down in the classroom. Ni Martin immediately pulled back.

As soon as Madam dismissed us, I rushed out. I too had seen him looking through the glass window. That was not the first time my brother was peeing through the window of our classroom. He always did so whenever they were let out before we were, for either Long Break or the close of school for the day.

However, this particular long break, we both had every reason to look forward to each other. We were both very hungry. This was because we had not eaten before leaving home. My brother and I had been selling 'akra' before leaving for school. Although the sale was nothing new to our daily routine, since our elder sister, Ma Marty always 'fried' akra' for us to sell to employees at the nearby Agric Farm as it was called, this particular day was different. For some reasons there were lots of buyers and consumers of our sister's food. As a result, my brother and I decided to delay and sell everything if possible. We did. But then, the price we had to pay was leaving for school without eating breakfast. To remedy the situation, our mothers combined the breakfast and our usual packed launch and put them in our school food bag. We were then to eat the food at Long Break.

So, when I stepped out of the classroom, Ni Martin immediately reacted:

"What took you so long? I've been waiting for a long time!'

"It's the teacher." I said. "She made us work for very long."

Together as usual, we stepped on to the earthen passage that led from the Infants 1 A and Infants 1B block to Infants 2A and 2B building. We were heading for the stone wall behind which we, like many other children, kept our sacks of food each day we came to school and then collected them to eat on the nearby football pitch at Long Break. However, the way to the stone wall went in the direction opposite to the Infants 2A and 2B block. To attain the stone wall from our own building, one had to turn right and then take a sharp right towards the main entrance to the school. Then, a short distance away, the stone wall extended far to the left and to the right.

Our hunger was such that we felt irritated by the many other children who crowded in front of us as they too made their way to their food sacks and baskets. We felt that these other pupils were unnecessarily delaying us.

"I say, wuna pass me! Wuna pass me!" Ni Martin shouted in pidgin as he broke his way through the crowd and I followed closely in his footsteps.

That was not the first time I was walking behind my brother. He was three years my senior. He was bigger and stronger and always defended me when I was threatened by bigger boys. Once we had P.E. and I, like other boys, changed into my P.E. shorts. When it was time to change back into our uniforms, I discovered that another boy who had been changing next to me had swapped my brand new P.E. shorts for his old and faded ones. When I approached him, I was shocked by his response which was that the shorts he had were his. He and I were both in Infants 1B. To back his case, he fetched our Class Head Boy, who without investigating the matter, declared that the shorts were Angong's. I was so angered that I went and fetched my brother who was the Head Boy of Infants 1A. I was happy that Pius would find his match in Ni Martin. They were both tall, of heavy build and muscular.

Ni Martin's reaction when he saw the shorts I was holding was swift

"Those are not my brother's shorts!"

"How do you know that?" Challenged Pius.

"I know it because my brother's aren't this old. They're quite new."

"Then whose are they?" Pius asked defiantly.

"They are not mine! Angong has got my shorts and these are his." I said.

"That's not true! The shorts I have got are mine!" Angong retorted.

"Angong, you're not serious! Return my brother's shorts! Remove them! Take them off! You must..." My brother was lashing out.

"No, he won't. The shorts are his..." Pius said, pushing my brother.

A fight broke down between the two and within minutes, a crowd of cheering pupils had surrounded us. The next thing I knew was the headmaster, saying:

"What on earth is going on here?"

Immediately the cheering stopped and we all froze. The other children stepped aside as the headmaster, Mr Zama walked into the zigzag circle where my brother and Pius were fighting. But even they had stopped fighting. I felt my

137

blood freeze. At the N.A. school, we were all frightened of the headmaster because we knew he could be merciless when it came to caning.

"Are you two not Head Boys? Yet, you are fighting."

Before any of the fighters could say anything, the headmaster pressed the point:

"Go and wait for me in front of my office! And the rest of you, disperse!"

At once, we scattered in all directions, very happy we had been spared the cane.

I felt sorry for my brother and Pius because I knew nothing could save them from the headmaster's wrath. It was clear that since the headmaster had remarked that they were Head Boys, yet had fought, before asking them any questions, he would punish them for that fact first. Since it was Long Break and the children were playing all over the school compound, I decided to get nearer the headmaster's office. As I got near the office, I heard the headmaster saying:

"Why? Why did you do it? Why did you fight? What kind of example did you think you were setting? You, Martin, come over here and bend over. Let me start with you. I will give you and Pius twenty four strokes of the cane each." As each lash fell on my brother's buttocks, I screamed outside. That was just for the fighting. After that, Angong and I were sent for.

"Come in!" he barked, waving his cane violently at us.

"What is this I hear about a pair of shorts?"

No one was bold enough to respond.

"It's mine, sir." I responded, plucking up courage as the garment was mine after all.

"What happened to it?" he asked.

"Angong took it, sir."

"Angong!"

"Sir!"

"Have you got the shorts?"

"Yes, Sir."

"Why?"

"They're mine, sir"

"Pius, you're the Head Boy and I don't believe you can lie to me. Whose shorts are these? You tell me."

"Martin, whose are they?"

"They're Muma's sir."

"Muma, do you have any other pair of P.E. shorts?"

"Yes, sir. I have Angong's own…"

"They're not mine, sir. I have mine. I …" Angong countered.

"Shut up! Who asked you? Muma, carry on!"

"I have Angong's, sir. They're old."

"But at least, you have something to use. Since there is a deadlock here, I will conclude that you have P.E. shorts. Whether they're yours or not, that's beside the point."

"But my father will punish me, sir."

"Why will he?"

"Because I don't have my P.E. shorts, sir"

"But there's no conclusive evidence that the shorts are yours."

"But are they Angong's, sir."

"That may not be so, but he has the advantage that it is he who has them. That's to say that although there are two pairs of shorts in question, only one of them is claimed by both of you, and it's Angong who has that one. This case is therefore concluded. You may go home now."

Through this decision and despite Ni Martin's efforts, I lost my pair of shorts. Nonetheless, when I recalled the story to Pius some thirty years later, when the headmaster had departed from this world and the rest of us were already married with children, he made a joke about it and we both laughed. Then he added:

"The truth of the matter is that those brand new shorts were yours. I knew it all along. It was one of those things, you know."

I wished Angong and Ni Martin were present to hear this breaking news. But they were not. My brother was away, working in one of the provinces. As for Angong, I have never set eyes on him since the incident. In fact, at the end of that academic year, our school was closed down to make way for an agricultural college. We pupils went to other nearby schools.

***

Ni Martin crossed the road that ran right down the stone wall and separated that side of the wall from the classroom buildings and the football pitch. I followed him and as we got to where we had left our food sack, he suddenly stopped.

"Can you smell that, Muma?"

"Smell what?" I asked, surprised.

"Don't you smell anything? Something nice?"

"Something like what?" I inquired again as I moved towards him.

"I smelled fowl soup." He responded.

"Yes, you're right. I can smell it too." I concurred.

As I said so, I bent down to try to determine where the irresistible aroma was coming from. Ni Martin joined me. In front of us and lined against the wall were food sacks, baskets, plastic bags and boxes of all kinds. All of them contained food. Frustrated by our inability to find the sweet smelling chicken soup, we started opening the containers in order to get to the bottom of the matter. Fortunately, no on challenged us. At last we found the soup in a tied bundle of banana or plantain leaves that had first been warmed over a fire so that they were softer and malleable. In the same basket with the soup, was a bundle of achoo. Ni Martin, who had untied the soup, dipped his finger in it an cried out:

"The soup is too nice!"

140

Very quickly he tied back the soup and said to me:

"Muma, you pick up our food sack and put the chicken soup in it. Be quick before we get noticed." I tied it in a flash. In a minute we had climbed over the stone wall and already taken our usual place on the football pitch. Like other children who ate in pairs or groups, we had our own self-designated space on the pitch. Even so, not all children ate ion the pitch. Some ate across the road that separated the Infants 2A and 2B building with the Standard Six dormitory. Most children ate here and most of those who did so bought their food from the nearby cooked food open market that was authorized by the school and was run by a number of women from the neighbourhood.

My brother and I ate the fowl soup with our own roasted cocoyams and ripe pears that we had bought. It was such a delicious combination! We liked the fowl soup and the fowl itself so much that we even chewed and swallowed the bones. We also thoroughly licked the leaf in which the soup had been tied by repeatedly rubbing our forefingers against the remains of soup on the leaf and then licking our fingers. As soon as we finished eating, we joined our friends in a game of football. We were enjoying the game with my brother and I playing on the same side when all of a sudden a certain boy stepped on the pitch and demanded as he waved a food sack for us to see:

"Who get this sack? Who get this sack?"

"Na me! Na my sack!" answered my brother, running towards the boy.

"Na your sack?"

"Yes, I say na my sack"

"So na you tif my fowl soup?" The boy asked angrily. He then ran off with the sack, saying he was going to report to the headmaster. Fearing the consequences if the headmaster knew that we had stolen somebody's food, Ni Martin ran after the boy, pleading:

"Wait! I go tell you weti happen!"

But the boy was not listening as he ran off.

That same day the headmaster sent word round that he was convening an after-school assembly, which must be attended by all pupils and teachers. Such large assemblies took place on the football pitch and that was exactly where that day's one was held. Pupils lined up according to their classes with each teacher standing at the end of his or her formation. The headmaster spoke:

"Pupils, I want to talk to you today about a matter of grave concern. It has become clear to me that despite what we teach in this school about morals, some of you are still determined to be thieves, hardened criminals. During today's Long Break, my attention was drawn to the fact that some two boys deemed it fit to steal another boy's food and eat it. I have called this assembly because I want to teach the thieves an unforgettable lesson for themselves and for the rest of you. Martin Achiri and Muma Mokom, step out! I want four strong boys to come up and hold these thieves up so that I can personally cane them. They will each get thirty strokes of the cane."

As soon as I heard the number of strokes we were to get, I shuddered, for I knew that with that number of lashes from the headmaster, I would like in pain for a whole week. It had never happened to me but I knew other people who having received that number of strokes from Mr. Zama had been ill for days. As I stood awaiting my fate, tears rolled down my eyes. I turned and looked at my brother but found that his face was expressionless. That was not surprising because he had a heart that made him not to cry, regardless of whatever was done to him. Never before had I see him shed a tear.

"Who are the four boys coming out? You, Pius, Thomas Akum, Peter Tamasang and John Ndifor, come out and hold Martin up first!" The headmaster thundered.

The four boys tore their way through the sea of standing boys and girls, grabbed Ni Martin and held him out with his back facing up. Two of the boys each held an arm and the other two held a leg each. True to himself, he offered no resistance whatsoever, just as he had done when he was being thrashed after the incident involving the pair of shorts.

The headmaster spoke as the cane rose and fell:

"You… You… Martin have behaved very badly. You are a Head Boy and should know better. What kind of example do you think you are setting? You have disgraced your class…your teacher… your school … and your family."

When he had finished the job, he said to the four boys:

"Put him down. I hope that will teach him a lesson."

My brother walked away. He did not cry, he did not walk with difficulty and his eyes were not even red. It was now my turn. I closed my eyes. I yelled with each stroke that landed on my buttocks.

"Your crying won't help you, little thief. You were man enough to steal, or so you thought. Now you should be man enough to take your punishment. I thought…I thought…I thought you were a good boy, but what you have done… What you have done…What you have done has shamed me."

When it was all over, the headmaster ordered me to join my class. He re-iterated that the public chastisement was meant as a warning to us and the other children not to steal.

"Any child who steals again will get twice the number of strokes." He said as he dismissed us. That afternoon, my brother and I did not say much as we walked home. He tried to say one or two things but I didn't respond. I was in too much pain. Even so, little did we know what was awaiting us at home. No sooner had we branched off the main road into the narrow one that led into our compound than we saw our little four-year-old sister running towards us and looking anxious.

"Papa will beat you people! Papa will beat you! He has prepared a cane!"

"Why?" We both asked.

"Somebody told him you stole at school."

"Who? Who told him?" Ni Martin asked.

"I don't know." Mah answered.

As we walked up into the compound, we prepared our minds, although I must say my heart was pounding. As we got nearer, I saw my father pacing up and down and waving a cane as he spoke angrily, apparently more to himself than to anyone else. At once, I knew he was in a very bad mood and would unfailingly use the cane on us. The die was cast and our fate was sealed.

"Come this way, you thieves!" he yelled out when he noticed us. As we approached him he rushed at us and grabbed Ni Martin by the hand.

"You, come here!" He said to him

Turning to me, he grabbed my ear and roared:

"And you little rogue! Where do you think you're going?" I tried to mutter an answer but he hushed me down:

"Shut up! Not a word from you!"

I fell silent. When our father was angry with any of us, we knew it was best to talk as little as possible, even if it meant answering his questions with silence. The more we talked, the more he beat us. We also knew that when we were before him for trial, it was better for us to quickly get him in the anger mood, if we could, so that we could get the beating over and done with. This was the technique we adopted on the day we came home after stealing the fowl soup.

So after Pap had asked us one or two questions without obtaining any reply, he flew into a rage and gave us a serious thrashing. As my mother heard me yelling, she too came out crying and begged my father to leave it at that.

"Woman, if you say one more word, I'll beat you too." He gnarled. Upon those words, my mother promptly retreated into the house, crying and saying: "My child! My child!"

Ni Martin's mother did not come out. I guess it was because unlike me, he was not shouting out for help. Again, my brother was taking his share of the beating stoically.

The consequences of the thrashings our father gave us were grave. His cane left weals on our backs. We found that we could not go to school for eight days. So great were the pains we felt! Surprisingly, he never asked us on any of the days we stayed at home why we had not gone to school. My guess is that either he knew the thrashing had left us ill or our mothers had explained the situation to him. On the other hand, our mothers were always by our side tending our wounds, bathing us, feeding us, and generally keeping us company. Our six sisters and five brothers were also very sympathetic.

For our part, we vowed to each other, never again to take anything that did not belong to us without the expressed authorization of the owner. To this day, we have not broken the unwritten rule.